Wyckford G...

Small-town med...

There must be something in the water in
Wyckford, Massachusetts. The small and quirky
town is brimming with dedicated medics and first
responders who are at the top of their game.

The one thing they don't have is love. Some
have had it and then lost it, some wanted to find
themselves first and some have never felt they
could have it—until now. They're all about to find
themselves fighting to resist temptation—the
temptation to have everything they've ever wanted!

Discover Brock and Cassie's story in
Single Dad's Unexpected Reunion

Read Tate and Madi's story in
An ER Nurse to Redeem Him

Both available now!

And look out for the other
Wyckford General Hospital stories

Coming soon!

Dear Reader,

Welcome back to Wyckford! Book two in the series features fearless ER nurse Madison Scott and her journey to HEA with temporary flight paramedic Tate Griffin. As with most things in life, the best opportunities sometimes happen in the most unlikely places, and that's the case with these two. From their first sizzling connection during a nor'easter to pumpkin carving contests and a cranky old man at the free clinic, this book has it all. A sunshine, strong heroine. A brooding, wounded hero. Plus, appearances by all your favorite quirky characters from book one, too. I hope you enjoy reading *An ER Nurse to Redeem Him* as much as I enjoyed writing it!

Until next time, readers...

Happy reading!

Traci <3

An ER Nurse
to Redeem Him

TRACI DOUGLASS

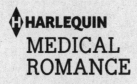

HARLEQUIN
MEDICAL
ROMANCE

HARLEQUIN®
MEDICAL ROMANCE™

Recycling programs for this product may not exist in your area.

ISBN-13: 978-1-335-59536-2

An ER Nurse to Redeem Him

Harlequin Enterprises ULC
22 Adelaide St. West, 41st Floor
Toronto, Ontario M5H 4E3, Canada
www.Harlequin.com

Printed in U.S.A.

Traci Douglass is a *USA TODAY* bestselling romance author with Harlequin, Entangled Publishing and Tule Publishing and has an MFA in Writing Popular Fiction from Seton Hill University. She writes sometimes funny, usually awkward, always emotional stories about strong, quirky, wounded characters overcoming past adversity to find their forever person and heartfelt, healing happily-ever-afters. Connect with her through her website: tracidouglassbooks.com.

CHAPTER ONE

TATE GRIFFIN JERKED upright in bed, breath seizing in his chest as jagged lightning bolted across the sky. Sweating and trembling, he scrubbed his hands over his face, then shoved off the covers. The chilly night air, made chillier by the rare, raging mid-October nor'easter outside, cooled his heated skin. He fought the urge to fall back to sleep because if he did, he'd be right back there again, smack in the middle of the nightmare that had dogged him for four years now. But as he stared into the rain-lashed darkness the memories returned anyway.

"We can't get any lower!" the pilot yelled as the UH-60 Black Hawk tilted precariously above the churning Indian Ocean. *"It's too dangerous!"*

Three stranded airmen depended on his team to rescue them.

"We can't leave them!" Tate shouted back. *"No one else will get here in time!"*

Ten seconds later, lightning cracked and towering waves slashed the bottom of the helicopter, causing it to shake violently. Close. Too close. A *sharp blast of light, followed by intense heat and excruciating pain, then...*

Nothing...

Tate stared over at his window as raindrops pelted the glass and forced himself to take a deep, shaky breath. He wasn't trapped in the burning wreckage of that downed chopper anymore, choking on seawater and the horrible knowledge he was the only survivor.

He hadn't saved a single soul that night. In fact, his fateful decision to even go on the mission had cost the lives of his team as well.

Back then, he'd been young and cocky. They all were. Tommy and Brad were pararescue like him, eager to save the world. Kelly was pararescue too, one of a small, elite group of women to graduate from an Air Force Special Warfare pipeline, qualifying as an STO—special tactics officer—by passing the grueling Apprentice Course at the service's Combat Control School at Pope Army Airfield. She'd done it in two attempts. It had taken Tate and the other guys at least three.

Kelly had been a force to be reckoned with, both on duty and off. She and Tate had even dated for a while, but in the end, they'd made better friends than lovers. He still missed her and the others on his crew every single day. Each time he boarded the helicopter at Wyckford General, he said a silent prayer for them. Then another for himself. That maybe someday he could atone for his failures.

Tonight, with the storm raging and his tension high, all the horrors of the accident seemed far too close to the peaceful, tiny tourist town of Wyckford, Massachusetts. He'd come here on extended leave from the Air Force after additional surgery on his leg to remove some scar tissue because he'd thought it might give him a chance to rest and heal, both mentally and physically. But he'd quickly gotten bored just sitting around on his butt and had ended up taking a temporary job as an EMT on the hospital's new flight crew, doing his level best to put one foot in front of the other and not get lost in the guilt and grief and shame living in his soul now because of the accident. Because in Tate's mind at least, it was his fault all those people were dead. And at night, when he was alone, there was too much space to think about everything he'd done wrong on that last mission and the burden he'd carried every day since.

The next streak of lightning and crack of thunder had him jumping out of his own skin again.

Christ.

Angry at his own weakness, Tate got up. No more eating lobster rolls before bed.

But if he was honest with himself, he knew it wasn't food that brought on those nightmares.

It was his PTSD from the accident. Another reason why staying busy was the best idea for him. When his friend Mark Bates—a firefighter in Wyckford—had first mentioned the flight EMT job, Tate had been skeptical and more than a little worried it might be too much for him. But when the past started haunting him more and more in the quiet, uneventful days, Tate had decided helping others was the least he could do to keep those ghosts at bay. Plus, working in the private sector turned out to be a nice change of pace from his usual highly regimented existence in the military.

Standing, Tate winced as he stretched his stiff leg, then pulled on a pair of jeans and tugged on his shirt from earlier before pulling on his socks and shoes. He'd rented this ranch-style house when he'd first arrived but hadn't really done much with it yet. He went into the living room and turned on the emergency scanner in the corner, figuring if he was up, he might as well make himself useful. Medical emergencies happened 24/7, regardless of the weather or location, so there was a good chance the flight crew could use an extra set of hands tonight.

In fact, maybe he'd just drive into town anyway. Stop at that little diner with the funny-looking bird on the sign on the way, if they were still open in the storm, and get some coffee to fully wake him up before going in.

Tate grabbed his jacket, then walked into the attached garage. As he flipped on the lights the smells of motor oil, well-greased tools and rubber tires welcomed him. In the center of the space sat his baby, his restored 1970 Chevelle SS454. The one luxury he afforded himself, his car brought back fond memories of working on vehicles together with his dad when Tate was growing up. Both his parents were gone now, so the car felt like a little piece of home.

He grabbed the keys from a peg on the wall and slid behind the wheel. The garage door lifted as the engine purred, and Tate backed out into the tempest, eager to outpace his past and pay his debt to all those lives lost on that fateful night four years ago.

The nor'easter raged as Madison Scott ran the short distance from her Mini Cooper to the front door of the Buzzy Bird Café. Thunder shook the ground, and the wind nearly blew her over. She'd forgotten an umbrella that morning because of course she had, but it was just as well—in these gales she'd probably have taken off like Mary Poppins anyway.

A bright bolt of lightning cleaved the ominous clouds, and Madi gasped as everything around her glowed like daytime for an instant: the parking lot, Buzzards Bay across the road full of angry roaring whitecaps and the menacing sky above.

Everything went dark again as she burst into the café, feeling like the hounds of hell were on her very tired heels. Her rubber-soled white nurse's shoes squeaked on the linoleum floor as she stood near the entrance to catch her breath.

The tiny seaside town of Wyckford tended to shut down after 10 p.m., and the diner was deserted except for Madi's best friend, Luna Norton, behind the counter. Luna's parents owned the café and Luna filled in part-time when needed and when it didn't interfere with her regular full-time job as a physical therapist for the hospital. She'd always reminded Madi of a fashion model, tall and leggy, not exactly beautiful, but with an interesting face that made you want to learn more about her. She was also a fantastic artist and had a fearless, kick-ass attitude to life in general. Tonight, her short black pixie cut was tousled and her gray eyes amused as she watched Madi make her way over to the counter.

"Nasty out there," Luna said. "Like a Stephen King novel or something."

Madi nodded as she shook off the icy rain from her scrubs. She'd forgotten a jacket too, having been on the go since dawn and in a perpetual rush for the whole day. One incredibly long ER shift and seventeen hours later, her clothes were now stuck to her like a second skin.

Another gale howled against the building and something heavy lashed the windows. Madi frowned, squinting back at the glass door. No. It couldn't be. Not five minutes ago it had been raining and now… *Snow*. Coming down fast and furious. "This weather's nuts. It's only October."

"That's New England for you," Luna said, her expression disgusted. "Sixty degrees this morning, thirty now. I never know how to dress this time of year."

Speaking of clothes, Madi really needed to change. She bit her lip and glanced out the door again. Maybe if she left now, she'd be okay.

As if reading her mind, Luna said, "Wait it out. This storm will blow over quick enough."

Madi knew better, but it was her own fault. She'd ignored the forecast ever since last week, when the weather guy had promised seventy-degree temps and the day hadn't gotten above fifty, leaving her to spend a long day frozen in the ER. Man, all she really wanted to do was to go home and go to sleep. "My house isn't far. I can make it, I think. I just need to pick up something for dinner first."

"Sorry." Luna hiked her thumb at the pass-through window showing a darkness beyond. "Grill's closed. I can make you a PB&J if you want."

Madi exhaled slow. Dead on her feet, she'd only stopped because she didn't want to cook that night. Or ever. She was horrible in the kitchen and could burn water. "Sounds good."

She took a seat at the counter while Luna gathered the ingredients and made sandwiches.

More lightning flashed, followed immediately by a thundering boom. Great. Now they had thundersnow. The entire diner shuddered under the blast of frigid winds. Then glass shattered as an ear-splitting crack sounded. A giant tree limb now waved at them through the new opening where the front door and windows had been moments before. Then the lights flickered and went out as another hard gust of wind sent more sharp shards tinkling to the floor.

Madi scurried to join Luna, who was crouched behind the counter. "We're safest right here, away from flying debris."

Luna swallowed audibly. "Maybe we should both leave now."

"No." Madi shook her head, staring through the shadows at the blocked entrance of the café. "It's not safe. Let's call for help though." She slapped her scrub pockets. "Damn. I left my phone in the car."

"I forgot mine at my apartment earlier when I changed," Luna said.

Huddled together in the dark, illuminated only by the battery-powered green exit sign over the back door in the kitchen, Madi said, "Too bad we don't have a big, strong hero who'll come looking for us."

Luna snorted. "Don't need one. I do my own heavy lifting."

Madi glanced at her friend's camo cargo mini-skirt, butt-kicking combat boots and snug long-sleeved tee. All topped by a bright pink apron with a cartoon buzzard on the front and the words Buzzy Bird Café emblazoned below it with their web address. One of Luna's designs, because on top of being a physical therapist and filling in as a waitress when needed, Luna was also a great artist. Madi would've been jealous if she didn't love her best friend so much.

She peeked over the counter again, hoping the snow had lightened up outside. It hadn't. In fact, the flakes were blowing sideways now, a constant icy bombardment against the remaining windows and flying in through the broken ones. Maybe if she went out through the rear exit, she could make her way around the building to get to her car. Madi peered up at the pass-through into the pitch-black space. Going through the obstacle course of the kitchen in the dark posed its own set of issues, but what else could she do? They couldn't just sit there all night and freeze to death.

Decision made, Madi climbed to her feet and started toward the swinging door into the back, only to halt as the sound of the two windows over the sink smashing echoed. Her heart stumbled. She sat back down beside Luna as the tree branch in the front entrance continued to wave at them tauntingly. Another escape attempt foiled.

The temperature inside the diner was dropping fast now as wind and snow gusted from two directions. Despite the situation, Madi was still starving. Her stomach growled, and Luna grabbed the sandwiches off the counter above them, handing one to her. They ate like it was their last meal, unnerved by the storm, huddled close to share body heat.

Eventually, Luna said, "If we survive this—"

"Hey." Madi scowled in concern. "We're going to be okay. As soon as the storm lets up, I'll get to my car and call for help, and—"

Luna shifted her weight. "Well, even so, once we get out of here, I'm going to change things. Live my life instead of letting it live me. I suck at that."

"Me too." Madi sighed. Growing up, she'd always been the stable one, the only child in her family who never caused drama, who always followed the rules, who didn't color outside the lines, who supported everyone else. And she did do all those things. She had her reasons, of course, but sometimes—like now—she wished she'd loosened a little, stopped worrying about being the glue at work, in her family. But seeing as how changing the world's perceptions of her would take a lot more than wishing and hoping, Madi decided to go with a more realistic request. "I'd just be happy with a date to the free clinic fundraiser next weekend. I'm the only nurse in the ER without one."

"Okay then." Luna pulled her order pad and

a pen from her apron pocket. "We're stuck here right now, so let's make a list of possible dates for you. And promise me you won't write off anyone too fast, even if he seems like Mr. Wrong."

Luna held out her pinkie for a swear. They'd done that since they were kids. Madi hooked little fingers with her bestie. "I promise—"

A loud thump sounded on one of the walls.

They went still, staring at each other with wide eyes.

"That wasn't a branch." A bad feeling came over Madi, the same one she got sometimes right before they got a serious incoming case. "It's a fist."

She rose to her knees and peered through the dim greenish light toward the direction where the sound had come from near the entrance. A snow drift now blocked the area. Incredible for this early in the season, but big, fat, round snow-flakes the size of dinner plates piled up fast she supposed.

The thump came again, along with a moan. A pained one.

Madi stood. "Someone's out there and they're hurt."

"It's too dangerous to go out there right now," Luna pleaded.

"I can't just ignore them." She sidled around the tree branches clogging the front door, arms wrapped around herself. Someone was in trouble, and it was her duty to help. The nurse's curse.

Glass crunched beneath her shoes, and snow blasted her in the face, making her shiver. Amazingly, the aluminum doorframe had withstood the impact, and she was able to shove her way outside. She peered into the parking lot but saw nothing.

"Hello?" Madi called, inching farther out into the night. "Is anyone—"

A hand grabbed her ankle, and she screamed as she fell into the darkness.

CHAPTER TWO

MADI SCRAMBLED BACKWARD, but a firm grip around her leg prevented her from going far. The hand was attached to a big male body, sprawled flat on his back. The guy shifted slightly and groaned, and Madi's panic turned to concern. She leaned over him, brushing the snow away from his face to get a better look, despite the pummeling wind. "Are you hurt?"

He didn't respond, wet from the snow and shivering beneath his down jacket. Blood trickled down his temple from a nasty gash over his right eyebrow. His eye was swollen too, probably from being struck by the tree that had fallen. Lightning flashed once more, and his eyes flew open, green-gold and intense, unwavering on hers.

She knew him. Tate Griffin, one of the flight paramedics at the hospital. All the nurses and half the doctors—both female and male—lusted after him because he was so handsome.

They'd never been formally introduced, but Madi had worked indirectly with him at Wyckford General. He'd started a few months back and generally kept to himself. He was always cordial and well-prepared when giving rundowns on patients to staff, at least from what Madi had seen of him.

She'd sighted him in town too—here at the Buzzy Bird, at the local gym, buying gas for his muscle car. Tall and broad shouldered. She remembered how the muscles of his back strained his T-shirt as he moved, how long his legs were, how he looked in his dark sunglasses, jaw firm and mouth grim, lending him a hint of brooding bad boy that had always intrigued Madi— probably more than it should. Still, a little frisson of female awareness always skittered up Madi's spine whenever she saw him and tonight was no exception, even when he was wet and cold and hurt beside her.

"It's okay," Madi said to him. "You were hit by a large branch. You'll need stitches. I can—"

Before she could finish, Tate caught her by the wrist and rolled her beneath two hundred pounds of solid muscle, the entire length of her pressed ruthlessly hard into the snow by him, her hands pinned high over her head by his. He wasn't crushing her, or hurting her, but his hold was effective. In less than a second, he'd immobilized her between the ground and his body.

"Who are you?" he growled, his voice low and rough, raising more goosebumps on her chilled flesh.

"Madison Scott, RN. We've seen each other in the ER." She struggled to free herself, but it was like moving against a slab of cement. "You have a head injury. And you're hypothermic."

His chest heaved against hers, his breathing too rapid. It was hard to see anything, but she'd bet good money he wasn't fully conscious at that point. His grip was still strong though. He felt much colder now, and if that big branch *had* hit him, then he more than likely had a concussion too, in addition to the cut on his head and his swollen eye. She stopped squirming beneath him. "We need to get you inside."

Slowly the man drew back, pulling off her until he was on his knees, but he kept hold of her wrists in one hand. His eyes were shadowed in the darkness, but his tension came through loud and clear.

"Are *you* hurt?" he asked, his tone sluggish.

Madi sat up. "No. I'm fine. *You're* bleeding and—"

Tate interrupted her with a mumbled denial, followed by another groan before he toppled again. Madi barely managed to break his fall with her own torso, and they both fell back into the snow.

"That's a lot of blood."

She peeked out from beneath Tate to see Luna's face wedged between the fallen tree branches and the doorframe.

"Can you help me get him into my car?" Madi tried to sit up again. "My phone's there, and I can turn on the heater to warm him up while we call 911."

Luna eased fully outside, then came over to peer into his face. "Oh, gosh! That's Tate Griffin. He's one of my physical therapy patients."

"Really? Well, we need to get him out of this weather." Madi finally managed to extract herself from beneath his heavy weight, then wrapped her arms around him from behind, lifting his head and shoulders out of the snow and into her lap. He didn't move.

"It's karma. You know that, right?" Luna took Tate's feet and together they huffed and puffed as they dragged him to Madi's car. "He could be your date. I don't know why I didn't think of him."

"The last thing I'm worried about at the moment is the auction."

Squinting into the wind, they made it to her Mini Cooper and, thankfully, the keys were still in the ignition. They got Tate loaded into the passenger seat, bending his long legs to accommodate his torso, then she climbed behind the wheel and started the engine. Once the car was running and the heat was blasting, she dug her phone out of the console and handed it to Luna while she checked Tate's vitals. "Have them send an ambulance. Tell them we've have a male, approximately late thirties, unconscious with a head injury and possible hypothermia."

"Fifteen minutes because of the weather," Luna

said after she ended the call, the snow glittering on her dark short hair making her look like a pixie. "They said to keep him warm and dry."

Madi nodded, then focused on her patient. Tate's brow was still furrowed and his expression troubled. Whatever he was dreaming about, it wasn't pleasant. Then his shoulders and neck tensed, and he went rigid. She cupped both sides of his face to hold him still, her voice soft and soothing. "Relax. Help is on the way."

He let out a low, rough wail. "They're gone. All…my fault."

"Shh." She knew not to wake him abruptly. "I've got you—"

Tate shoved her hand away and sat up fast, blinking at her, his gaze unfocused and filled with shadows.

"We've called an ambulance," she said, trying to keep him calm.

He swiped at his temple, then scowled at the blood on his fingers. "What the—"

"Stay still," she said, forcing him to lie back down.

"Bossy," he muttered, his eyes closing once more. "But hot."

Hot? Madi frowned down at her wrinkled scrubs and wet shoes. Her hair had to be a complete disaster by now. She was about as far from "hot" as a person could get, which only further confirmed his head injury in her mind. Madi looked down at Tate's handsome, bloody face, and remembered her promise to Luna earlier. She had to admit she could do worse for a date than Tate Griffin.

A female voice penetrated the haze in Tate's brain.

He took stock of himself before opening his eyes again. He wasn't dead. His legs ached from being stuffed into an awkward position in this tiny little clown car. He shifted slightly, but pain lanced through his skull. Nauseated, he licked his dry lips and tried to focus. "I'm okay."

"Stay still," the woman said, the same one who'd told him he'd been hit by a branch. It felt more like he'd been run over by a semi. Repeatedly. Her voice came from his left, so she must be sitting in the driver's seat. Despite the bile scalding his throat, Tate managed to squint one eye open to see her. Tricky, that, since everything was doubled. Brown hair, long and wet and currently scraggly. Purple scrubs embroidered with the Wyckford General Hospital logo over the pocket on her chest. *A very nice chest too.* Her face was pretty in an understated way, her features delicate but set with purpose. No pushover then. Probably a nurse.

Yeah. She'd told him that, he vaguely remembered. Mary? Milly? McKenzie?

His temples throbbed as he recalled it. Madison. Yep, that was it. Madison Scott, RN.

He'd seen her before on his EMT shifts. Cute, but bossy.

And if she wanted to talk shop, well, unfortunately, Tate had dealt with more head injuries than she could possibly imagine.

Still, her warm hand stroked the side of his face and felt better than anything had in a long time. He turned into it without thinking, trying to figure out how he'd ended up there. He remembered having his usual nightmare, then driving into town to see if they needed him for a shift. Then the rain became snow, and everything went sideways. Literally. As conditions deteriorated into a blizzard, the lights of the diner had acted as a beacon. He'd parked safely and nearly made it to the door when something heavy slammed into him from behind and the world went black.

Unsettled, Tate tried to move, but Nurse Scott held him down. Focusing past the jackhammering in his skull was difficult, but if he squinted, the cobwebs in his vision weren't quite so bad. Behind her shoulder, another woman leaned over the backseat, staring at him. This face he knew. Luna, his physical therapist. He wondered what she was doing at the café on a night like this before he remembered she also worked here sometimes.

Tate gave in to the lethargy threatening to pull him under, sinking into her caring warmth. "Thanks for saving me, ladies."

Madison smiled down at him and despite his

situation, a tingle of awareness spiked through his bloodstream. "The ambulance will be here soon. You've had quite a night."

So have you. He saw it in his nurse's pretty chocolate-hued eyes.

"They'll patch you up and get you some meds for your pain," she continued.

"No narcotics," Tate said, then gripped his aching head to keep it from flying off his shoulders. Stars danced in front of his eyes, turning to red and blue lights.

Madi looked down at her patient again. His complexion had gone a bit ashy beneath his light brown skin. Clammy too, but he was conscious. The ambulance pulled up near the Mini and two EMTs got out, then walked to the back of the rig for their gear and a gurney.

"What happened?" Tate ground out, his jaw tight, his big body a solid weight beside her.

Memory loss wasn't uncommon after head trauma. "Tree on the head."

"And my friend here came to your rescue," Luna told him. "You owe her a favor."

"Luna!"

"She needs a date this weekend," Luna continued as if Madi hadn't spoken. "If you go with her to her charity event on Saturday night, you'd save her from merciless ridicule, so…"

Madi sighed. "This is completely inappropriate and—"

"Okay," Tate mumbled.

Wide-eyed, Madi looked at her patient, then Luna again. She normally dated men who were fine. Fine looking, fine acting, just all-around fine. No one to rock the boat. No one to cause disruptions to anyone else's lives or their perceptions of little "Miss Goody Two-Shoes"—a nickname she'd earned as a kid and still despised to this day. Fine was good. Fine was safe. Fine seemed to be her lot in life.

But Tate Griffin was *so* not her usual type. He was the kind of man who'd create waves in town if the two of them were seen dating. But Wyckford better hold on to their proverbial hats because it looked like they would indeed be going on a date together, even if it was fake. And if Tate looked this good while bleeding and semi-conscious, Madi could only imagine what he'd look like on his feet and dressed to the nines.

CHAPTER THREE

ONE WEEK LATER, Madi still walked around in a cloud of nervous anticipation. The charity auction was that night, and she'd spent the last seven days alternating between long ER shifts and working on the event. A large portion of the evening's proceeds would go toward her beloved Health Services Clinic where anyone in the county could go to get free medical treatment, community recovery resources, teen programs, crisis counseling and a whole host of other things. Hopefully, the money raised would keep them going until next year. It's what should have been foremost in her mind.

Instead, her thoughts kept returning to Tate Griffin.

She'd hoped to touch base with him at least once—either on a shift or around town—so they could work out the details of tonight, but, so far, he hadn't made an appearance. Then again, given his injuries that night, he'd probably been put on bed rest for a few days. It was possible he hadn't been cleared for duty yet. Whatever the cause,

Madi hadn't gotten his phone number. And because Tate hadn't technically been her patient, looking up his files from the other night now would be a HIPPA violation. So, if she wanted his information, she'd have to ask for it. But with the rumor mill inside the hospital and in the town in general, that just wasn't an option. The two of them together at the auction would create a big enough stir tonight. She considered asking Luna but didn't want to add any more fuel to the fire. He'd be there, and if not, well, she'd survive. She'd survived much worse, after all.

Luckily, Madi had a full patient roster that day to keep her busy and stop her from spiraling into an anxious mess about the evening. Including a new arrival in the ER—a crotchety old man named Luther Martin. He had an arrhythmia complicated by vasovagal syncope, which caused dizziness and fainting. He also suffered from a terminal meanness.

"I brought your juice," she said, entering Mr. Martin's room.

"I asked for it three hours ago. What's wrong with you? You were always slower than molasses."

Madi ignored his complaint because it had been five minutes since he'd asked. And because he'd been her first-grade teacher at Wyckford Elementary thirty years prior, before he'd retired. The man was so difficult that even his own son, who lived an hour away in Boston, refused to call or visit.

"I remember you wet your pants in front of the whole class, missy," Mr. Martin said. "Don't act all superior with me now."

She'd been six at the time, but her face still heated with remembered shame. "Because you wouldn't let me go to the bathroom."

"Recess was five minutes away."

"I couldn't wait."

"So, you're making *me* wait now? You're a horrible nurse, letting what happened back then affect your treatment of me."

Madi could have argued she was the only one on staff willing to help the old coot, but she took the high road and set the cup, complete with straw, on Mr. Martin's bedside tray.

He picked it up, sniffed, then took a tiny sip, acting like it was radioactive waste. "I wanted *apple*."

"You asked for cranberry."

Mr. Martin cursed loud and threw the juice against the wall. The liquid splashed across the bedding, the floor, the IV pole, and Madi. Juice dripped off her nose, and she sighed. It took her and housekeeping twenty minutes to clean up the mess. Ten more to get the patient back into his freshly made bed. She huffed with the effort.

"Out of shape or just gaining some weight?" he asked, his tone snide.

Madi reminded herself she helped save lives, not take them, and walked out of the room.

Thankfully, a new patient came into the ER to distract her, a two-year-old with a laceration requiring stitches. Madi got him cleaned up and prepped the area for the doctor—lidocaine, a suture kit, four-by-fours—then assisted in the closing of the wound.

The rest of her morning followed much the same pattern.

At noon, she went to the staff break room and grabbed her lunch from the fridge. Her older sister, Toni, was there too. Once upon a time, Toni had been wild. So had her other two siblings: Jack Jr. and Karrie, Toni's twin. Madi had always been the good one, hoping to stand out.

Then, the one time when her goodness and support could've have made the difference between life and death, she'd failed. The night Karrie had taken a lethal dose of pills and died. Even all these years later, Madi felt guilty about it. If she'd just listened more, paid more attention to her, given her the support she'd needed, maybe Karrie would still be alive. It didn't matter that Madi had only been sixteen at the time and Karrie was eighteen and a lifetime apart experience-wise.

Some people might have gone the opposite route after that—drinking and partying to bury the hurt and pain and guilt. That's what Toni and Jack Jr. had done. But Madi had instead grown more terrified to do anything wrong, to screw up again and lose more people she loved. For all the good it did. Her parents had ended up divorced anyway, with her father moving to Hawaii and having no communication with the family again. Still, she was undeterred. Being good and dependable and supportive was who she was now, for better or worse. And if she sometimes wanted to break free of that, well, it was a nice fantasy, but she had a lot riding on her persona these days. Including the fate of her beloved clinic. She hoped it was enough to keep the lights on for another year.

Madi took a seat beside Toni at the large round table in the center of the break room, stopping to wave at Lucille Munson, one of the elderly volunteers from the local retirement home, who sat on a sofa along the wall sipping a cup of tea. No one knew exactly how old Lucille was, but before moving into Sunny Village, she'd run the town's art gallery. She was also a hub of all things gossip in Wyckford with Ben Murphy, the father of Madi's other best friend, Cassie Murphy. Cassie was a surgeon and had recently moved back to town from San Diego to be with Brock Turner, the resident GP and pediatrician.

Their second chance at romance gave her hope maybe she'd find her special someone someday too. If she was honest, that was what she wanted most, deep down inside.

Toni smiled and put down her phone. "Hey, sis. Heard you have a date to your event tonight."

Frowning, she froze as she pulled out her sandwich. "How did you hear that?"

"I'm psychic." Her sister stole Madi's chips from her lunch bag.

"Luna told you, didn't she?"

"Yep. When I grabbed breakfast at the café earlier." Toni munched away. "Can't believe you landed Tate Griffin."

Madi glanced around, all too aware of the other staff probably hanging on their every word.

"Seriously. I'm impressed. The last guy you dated was a boring accountant from Providence." Toni laughed loudly, looking over at the sofa where Lucille was almost falling out of her seat trying to hear their conversation. "Are you catching all of this?"

"I am." The elderly woman pulled out her cell phone and started typing. "Good stuff. Keep going."

After her shift, Madi drove home and fed the ancient black cat who'd come with the house she'd inherited from her grandmother, the one who answered only to "Violet" and only when food was involved. Before she got ready for the charity event, Madi checked her social media—then wished she hadn't.

Because of course Lucille had tagged her in a post to the town's Facebook page.

Tonight's the big dinner and auction with all proceeds going to support the Health Services Clinic, organized by Wyckford General's own Madison Scott, ER nurse extraordinaire, who apparently has a date with...flight paramedic Tate Griffin!

P.S. If anyone snaps pictures of the couple tonight, please share here.

CHAPTER FOUR

TATE'S ROUTINE HADN'T changed much since he'd come to Wyckford. He got up in the mornings and worked out, either by swimming—when it was nice enough—or going to the gym, usually with Mark and sometimes Brock Turner, though he didn't come with them often anymore. Brock had gotten engaged a few months back to Cassie Murphy, a big-time surgeon who'd come back home to consult on a case. They'd supposedly found their happily-ever-after together.

If you went in for that sort of thing.

Tate didn't, but it was fine. He preferred keeping things light and friendly without too many messy connections. Connections only caused pain and suffering when they were gone, in his experience. Just look at his team, his parents. So yeah. He had lots of casual friends and a few best buds. Mark Bates was one of the latter. He'd moved to Wyckford from Chicago after his discharge from the Navy, so they had the military in common. He'd been the only person Tate knew in town when he'd arrived. And the first person to give him a run for his money at the gym too.

Today was warm for October, so Tate went swimming alone since Mark was busy. He put on his wet suit and used a small private beach not far from his rental house on Buzzards Bay, doing laps until exhaustion nearly pulled him under. Then he forced himself to walk along the rocky shore for about a mile. At first, it was slow going, more like a crawl, but he went the distance, no problem. Quite the feat, given that four years ago he'd had a severe post-surgical infection in his leg after the helicopter crash. And while overall he'd recovered well from the ordeal within a year, except for a permanent slight limp, he'd had surgery a few months back to remove some excess scar tissue, thus this new leave from the Air Force. But things were improving daily and hopefully he'd be cleared to return to duty soon. He was building up his strength and endurance.

He should be grateful he still had a leg at all after the accident. And honestly, even if he'd had an amputation, it would still have been a far better outcome than the fate of the rest of his team that night. They'd lost their lives.

Why didn't I just postpone that flight a few hours? Wait for the storm to pass? Wait until daylight?

He knew the answer to those questions. They'd been stated clearly in black-and-white by the naval investigators who'd cleared him of any wrong-doing in that night's horrendous accident. Post-poning the rescue would have been an absolute death sentence to the airmen trapped in the ocean. The cyclone hadn't passed for another day, and daylight wouldn't have helped anything in the sit-uation, other than making it even more apparent what a dire mess it had been. His crew hadn't hesitated to follow him into the breach. They'd made their choice.

Now he had to live with the consequences.

Tate knew all of this, but still grief and guilt slashed through him again. He stopped to catch his breath. He hadn't saved any of them. Not his team. Not the victims. No one. Despite all his training as a trauma paramedic, despite all his pararescue skills, despite all of it, he'd failed. He'd always prided himself on being a good leader—respon-sive, supportive, making the difficult decisions. But the accident had made him doubt everything.

So now, he worked twice as hard as everyone else on the crew at the hospital, double- and triple-checking it all to make sure he didn't screw up again. It was also why he kept the circle of people he let close to him small. Because if he couldn't protect those he cared for, what was the point? It felt like penance—the long hours, the lonely nights—because maybe if he punished himself enough, saved enough people, perhaps he could somehow earn the forgiveness of those he'd failed all those years ago.

Even if he'd never forgive himself.

Once he got back from his swim, Tate changed out of his wet suit, showered, then stared in the mirror, barely recognizing the man looking back. Brock had done his recheck from the head injury and mild concussion after the storm and had cleared him to return to the flight crew. But it took a bit to get back in the regular shift rotation, so Tate had mainly spent the week stuck at home, getting more restless by the second. Another reason he was glad to have an excuse to get out of his house tonight, beside the fact he had a date with Nurse Scott from the parking lot.

Was she as pretty as he remembered from that night or was that just another hallucination courtesy of the bump on his head? If Tate shut his eyes, he could still remember how she'd smelled, like bleach and flowers and crisp snow from the weather.

Enough.

Shaking off the silly thoughts, Tate stared in the mirror again and reminded himself this was a favor for her helping him that night, nothing more.

Even so, he looked a mess—as his mom used to say—with stitches over one eye and a yellowing bruise on his cheek from the tree branch that had hit him upside the head. His hair was on the wrong side of a haircut, and he'd skipped shaving that morning. He'd lost some weight too, making the angles of his face starker. His eyes looked… *hollow*.

There was no way cute, kind Nurse Scott wanted anything more than a favor from him tonight. She'd been a Good Samaritan who'd helped him when he needed it. That was all. This wasn't some grand romance. It was a business arrangement. Because while his body might have mostly recovered from the accident, there was work yet to do on his soul.

Without thinking he grabbed the empty bottle of Vicodin on the vanity and rolled it between his fingers. He'd quit cold turkey three years ago the minute he recognized his desperation to numb everything, but the craving remained. The pills made it all go away.

He finished getting dressed, then went out to his garage and the Chevelle.

The rest of the day passed with him under the chassis since he didn't have a shift that day. He thought about stopping by the hospital to see if he could find Madison and discuss their plans tonight, but then decided against. He was currently filthy again from working on the Chevelle's transmission. Plus, there really wasn't a reason to see her beforehand. He'd seen the flyers plastered all over town about the auction, so he knew where to be and when.

No sense making a bigger deal out of this than

it was. Regardless of how his body reacted each time he remembered sitting beside her in that tiny car, the way her breath had hitched as she tenderly stroked his hair, her chocolate-brown eyes and her parted pink lips…

"Stop it, son." His dad's voice rang through his head, giving Tate advice when he was unsure about something. *"Mind on your work and hands busy. Stay out of trouble, and you'll be just fine."*

After several hours more under the car, he finally rolled out on the creeper, rubbing his left thigh absently, determined to keep his end of the deal he'd made with Madison that night. It would be okay. They'd have a nice dinner, maybe he'd bid on some stuff at the auction since the proceeds went for a good cause, and then he'd come home and sink into his comfortable routine again.

No harm, no foul. His stupid reactions and thoughts about the sexy nurse would be over.

All he needed to do was make it through the next couple of hours with his head on straight and his heart tucked away safely where he'd locked it four years ago.

Resolved, he went back inside and showered again, then dressed in his best suit, before checking the clock and slipping his keys, cell phone, and wallet into his pocket and walking out to the Chevelle.

Tate had a fake date to keep.

* * *

Madi paced the lobby of the town's 1920s-era restored theater-turned-event-space in her little black dress and heels, nodding to the occasional late-arriving straggler. Through the doors into the large gathering room, the delicious smells of dinner made her antsy to get in there with her guests—to eat, smile, schmooze. Her job tonight was to get people fired up to donate and bid. But she was still missing her escort for the evening.

She'd been certain Tate would come, even though they'd not spoken since the night of the storm. After all, the charity auction was the hopping place to be. Well, she wasn't giving up hope yet.

It was all Luna's fault, Madi decided. Making her pinkie swear. Tate was hot and had that restless, brooding air about him that lit her up from the inside out for some reason. She'd never taken a walk on the wild side before, but he did make it look extremely appealing...

Whoops. No.

She quickly reeled those errant thoughts in fast. They barely knew each other. *Gah!* All this stress and nervousness was exactly why she didn't date outside her safe box of accountants and bankers. She should have never made that stupid pinkie swear.

"Hey," Luna said, coming up to Madi in the lobby.

Madi blinked at her best friend's appearance. Luna looked amazing, dressed to perfection with her hair and makeup done. Her slinky purple dress emphasized her curves and long legs, as did her stiletto heels. "Wow."

"Thanks." Luna shrugged, then looked away fast as Mark Bates walked by and waved to Madi.

Usually, the guy was in full firefighter gear. But tonight, Mark looked dapper in his suit. Six foot and rangy, the tailoring showed off his lean, muscled form, and the dark charcoal fabric highlighted Mark's sun-kissed blond surfer looks and light blue eyes. He flashed an easy smile as he passed, straight white teeth gleaming against his tanned skin. "Hey."

"Hey," Madi said.

Then he glanced at Luna, his eyes widening.

She kept her attention on Madi. "See you in there."

Mark watched Luna vanish into the gathering room, and Madi bit back a grin. The poor guy looked bewildered. Sharp, quick-witted, and tough as hell, he was one of five firefighters on the Wyckford brigade and handled everything from Jaws of Life rescues to removing kittens from trees. Nothing much ever seemed to rattle him.

Until tonight, apparently.

He shook his head as he walked off.

Alone once more, Madi looked around the lobby again. She'd been so busy earlier setting up and greeting people, maybe Tate had slipped in without her seeing him. But wouldn't he have come up to her and said hello at least? Ugh. This whole idea had been crazy from the start and reminded her of why she preferred her nice quiet life. It was predictable. Peaceful.

And boring.

Shaking her head at her own silliness, Madi walked over to peer out the large windows into the night, but there was no sign of Tate Griffin or his car. With a sigh, she squared her shoulders, then peeked inside the gathering room doors.

They had a sold-out crowd.

She wasted another five minutes tidying the already immaculate auction item displays on the table lining the back wall of the lobby, dawdling in front of a small silver bracelet. Each charm was handmade and unique to Wyckford in some way: a tiny buzzard, a miniature pier, a little fishing boat and an anchor. Normally, Madi only wore the infinity necklace her sister Karrie had given her. But this piece urged her to spend money she didn't have.

"Not exactly practical."

Mr. Martin stood behind her, leaning heavily on a cane, his wizened features twisted into an unfriendly smile.

Ignoring his statement, Madi asked instead, "Are you feeling better?"

"My ankles are swollen, my fingers are numb,

and I'm plugged up beyond any Roto-Rooter help."

As a nurse, Madi was used to people telling her things they'd never mention in polite conversation. "Well, please stay hydrated. Are you taking your meds?"

"There was a mix-up at the pharmacy."

"Did you call Dr. Turner?"

"I tried. He's an idiot. And he's twelve. Tries to skate by on his looks and reputation alone." Mr. Martin sniffed. "Not like his father."

Brock was not, in fact, an idiot. He was thirty-six, and one of the best MDs in Massachusetts. Plus, he'd worked his ass off to save the practice his father had started and was a good man to boot. He always helped Madi out at the clinic whenever he could. Of course, she might be a bit biased since he was also engaged to Cassie, but now wasn't the time or place to argue with the crotchety old man. "I'll check into the meds issue for you first thing in the morning."

"See that you do." Mr. Martin glanced around, scowling. "Where's your date? Been stood up?"

Then, without giving Madi time to answer, he limped away.

She turned back to stare at the bracelet again. He'd been right about the jewelry though. It *was* impractical for a nurse. The charms would snag on everything from leads to the bed rails.

"Honey, what are you doing out here?" Her mother.

Ellen Scott was a nursing supervisor at the hospital. Tonight, she wore her Sunday best, a pale blue dress showing off an early season tan she'd gotten from her taking her breaks during the summer on the hospital's upper deck where the new medical flight service helicopter landed.

"Pretty," her mother said, looking at the bracelet. "I had the kitchen save your dinner for you. Dessert's next for the rest of us."

Her mom kissed Madi on the cheek, then returned to the event.

When the lights dimmed in the gathering room, and the PowerPoint presentation of the auction items started, Madi sneaked inside to take the only empty seat at one of the back tables. It was too dark to see the people sitting around her. To her left sat a man facing the slide show. She squinted at his profile. He seemed vaguely familiar, but before she could figure out from where, someone tapped her shoulder. "Madi, there you are."

She craned her neck and smiled as the lights came up again. "Hello."

"I've been looking everywhere for you." Judith Meyer was nursing director. "I'm glad you finally get a chance to rest and enjoy the fruits of your labor."

"Thanks. I made sure everything was ready out front. We have a full house. We're doing good."

Her boss grinned. "Fabulous! And how are you, Tate?"

Stunned, Madi whirled around to find him next to her in the left-hand chair, a bandage above one eye and the small bruise on his temple yellowish purple against his light brown skin. His green-gold eyes were as gorgeous as she remembered and were now lit with curiosity.

Wow.

A spotlight hit the stage and the MC announced, "And now, let's welcome the hardest-working nurse in Wyckford. Please give a round of applause for Madison Scott!"

CHAPTER FIVE

"GO ON." JUDITH GRINNED, nudging her from her seat before turning to Tate. "Escort your date up there."

"Oh," Madi rushed to cover. "It's okay, he doesn't have to—"

But Tate was already on his feet, his hand at the small of her back, gesturing for Madi to precede him, a smile curving his lips.

She did her best to exude confidence for anyone watching them—and *everyone* was watching them—then whispered to the man at her side, "I was worried you'd forgotten about me."

Something flickered in his eyes before he covered it and his polite mask fell into place. Madi wasn't sure how he'd managed to slip past her in the lobby without her seeing him, but it didn't matter. She was grateful Tate was willing to play her fake date in front of the whole town.

They threaded their way through the tables to the stage, the sea of faces nothing but a blur. All she could concentrate on was the big, warm hand at the small of her back attached to the gorgeous guy escorting her. Tate stood near enough now that his scent—woods and spice and everything nice—surrounded her. It nearly made her turn around and pull him away into a private corner where they could get to know each other better. A lot better.

But as they got to the stairs leading up to the stage, Madi forced herself to focus on the task at hand. The auction. Raising money for the clinic. That was way more important than her neglected libido right now. She glanced over at Tate then and noticed for the first time his slight limp. Huh. She didn't remember him having a leg injury the night of the storm. She frowned. "Are you okay?"

Rather than answering, Tate nudged her up the steps. "Go. People are waiting."

With five hundred sets of eyes on her, Madi took the stage and grabbed the mic from the MC. "Good evening."

The crowd cheered.

Madi gave a genuine smile at their enthusiastic greeting. She'd grown up here, worked here, lived here. Even if she somehow ended up on the other side of the world, she'd always be from Wyckford. "Thank you all for coming and supporting such a worthy cause. Now, let's make some money for our free clinic tonight, eh?" Madi pointed to the big screen behind her where pictures of the items were being displayed. "Everyone, get your paddles ready because we have some great things for you to buy. Our favorite auctioneer, Harry Langston, is here from Boston, and I expect to see lots of bidding action."

"Let your date say hello too!" Lucille called from a table near the front, interrupting her. Dressed in a silver gown that resembled a disco ball, the older woman snapped a photo of Madi and Tate with her phone, then winked.

As Tate reached over to grab the mic, their fingers brushed and made her shiver. "Hello," he said, winking back at Lucille. "I'm Tate Griffin. The…date."

"And there you have it." Madi commandeered the microphone again, not wanting to give the old busybody even more to gossip about online. "Now let's get to the auction and have a good time."

After introducing the auctioneer, they stepped off stage again, Madi focused on returning to their table and eating her dinner now that her speech was over, but she was waylaid by her mom, who pulled her down for a hug. Tate seemed to have disappeared, which was just as well because she wasn't sure she was up for answering any more questions about him just then.

Bidding began with her bracelet, and Madi quickly grabbed a paddle from her mom's table, considering it a sacrifice for the cause.

That's what she told herself anyway.

Someone else eventually won, and the auctioneer moved on to the next item.

"You did a great job tonight, honey." Her mother squeezed her hand, eyes suspiciously damp. "Out of all my kids, you've always been the good one. Running the clinic, organizing this auction. I'm so proud of you!"

They hugged again and Madi was glad for the support. "Thanks."

"Where's your date?" her mom asked, searching behind Madi. "I've seen him around the hospital. He seems like a nice young man. If a bit quiet and mysterious. How did you two meet?"

Nice wasn't the first word that popped into Madi's head when she thought of Tate.

"Oh, look. Here he comes now." Her mother beamed at someone over Madi's shoulder. Tate, of course, returning with two glasses of wine. He handed one to Madi.

"I'm Ellen Scott, Madi's mother." She held out her hand.

"Tate Griffin," he said, shaking her hand. "Pleasure, ma'am."

"I love your accent," her mother said. "Where are you from?"

"All over really." Tate sipped his wine. "My dad was in the Air Force. But we spent the most time in Louisiana when I was growing up. Barksdale AFB. Guess I brought a bit of the south with me."

"I'd say so." Her mother was a shameless flirt. Madi secretly wished she had even half of the woman's skills in that department, but she hadn't inherited that gene, apparently. When it came to social interactions, most people described her as sweet and kind and polite, but not flirty. Her mother patted Tate's hand. "You are a charmer, aren't you?"

"Mom!" Madi scolded, her face heating. The last thing she needed now was Tate thinking this was a setup for more than just the one evening. And while she wouldn't be opposed to seeing him again after tonight, she wouldn't go there.

"What?" Her mother smiled. "Fine. Well, you two have a good time. I need to start spending some money."

Tate looked at Madi, giving her a sardonic half toast with his glass. "Cheers."

They both returned to their own table. Madi caught one of the wait staff and had them bring out her dinner that had been held in the kitchen for her. While she ate her yummy baked chicken and veggies, she monitored the room around her. The space was filled with happy, well-fed people, but they seemed to be doing more socializing than buying. When a Patriots game package came up and no one lifted their paddle, Madi's heart sank. And when a bid did finally come in, it was far less than expected.

The next item was another big-ticket one—an expensive night on the town in Boston, including a limo, a fancy dinner and an orchestra concert. The bids started low again. They had to do better.

Three-quarters of their budget for the free clinic came from these donations.

Then Tate offered two hundred dollars higher than the previous bidder.

Madi stared at him. "What are you doing?"

He eyed her with a wicked, devious smile. And when someone joined him in a bidding war from across the room, Tate continued raising his paddle. Unbelievably, the battle for the "Night on the Town" continued for five more minutes, until the final sum was nothing short of dazzling.

Tate won.

Apparently satisfied, he set down his paddle and stretched his long legs out in front of him to watch the proceedings. Madi should have been watching the auction too, but now she couldn't take her eyes off him as the night kicked into full gear. The whole place went crazy, everyone bidding on all the items, playfully outdoing each other.

It was...*wonderful*.

But she couldn't stop thinking about how much money Tate had spent to get it going. She wasn't sure what a flight paramedic's salary was, especially a temporary one, but she didn't think it was enough for him to have that kind of extra cash just lying around. "What are you going to do with that package you won?"

"Have a night on the town, apparently." He

grinned at her, then hiked his chin toward the front of the room. "Trouble at six o'clock."

Lucille again, this time with another older gal from the retirement home's blue-haired posse. They both bid fiercely for the next auction item— a date with Arthur Schmidt, the elderly owner of the local hardware store.

"That guy has got to be ninety, right?" Tate frowned, watching them up their offers alarmingly. "Can he handle that much excitement?"

Thankfully, the auctioneer suggested the two women share the date, and things ended peacefully.

Tate winced in clear sympathy for Arthur, who now had not one, but two, dates.

"Don't feel sorry for him," Madi said. "Yes. In fact, Arthur's probably loving it."

He slid her a look. "Seriously?"

"Oh, yeah." Madi couldn't help laughing at the shocked look on Tate's face. "Sex doesn't stop just because you get older."

"I suppose it doesn't." Then Tate's gaze dropped from Madi's eyes to her mouth, and suddenly she felt like climbing into his lap and kissing him silly. Which was totally unlike her. But then, this whole night seemed like something out of a wacky rom-com movie, so…

Madi hadn't realized how much she'd leaned into him until she nearly fell against his chest. She quickly straightened and sipped her wine before laughing low. He was good. Really good. *Charmer indeed.* "Save the flirting for my mother. I'm immune."

He gave her a long look, then said, "Okay. But explain something to me. How does a woman like you not have a real date tonight?"

She blinked at him, part stunned, part sad. "Suffice it to say I work a lot."

"I've seen that," Tate said, still watching her with those too-perceptive green-gold eyes.

Madi reached for her wine, wishing it was something harder.

Tate's hand sat beside hers on the table, and as she watched, his thumb glided over her fingers, a small, casual touch that sent a naughty shudder of awareness through her. His dark brows drew together as he stared down at their hands, the air between them shimmering with possibilities as his tone shifted from flirty to something far more raw and real. "I've been known to work too much myself. It's a good way to escape."

Unsure how to respond to that, Madi sipped more wine, watching him over the rim of her glass. He was so close now she felt the warmth of his breath at her temple. In the crowded space, their nearness was no different from any other couple in the room, but butterflies swarmed inside her.

CHAPTER SIX

TATE HAD NO idea what he was doing, opening up to Madison Scott.

Getting in way too deep, way too fast, that's what.

Which was not like him at all. He was not a sharer, as his previous partners had always told him. Flirting was one thing. A distraction. A diversion. It came second nature to him. He used it like a shield to keep anyone from seeing what a complete mess he really was. But somehow, Madi seemed to cut through all his BS and get right to the heart of him. Scary, that.

And oddly exhilarating too.

She looked amazing tonight. Her deceptively modest black dress had little crisscross straps across her back and fell to midthigh, molding her curves and making him want to see more. High, strappy heels emphasized a world-class set of legs he'd only ever seen hidden beneath scrubs. And her hair, twisted up in some loose bun with a few tendrils falling around the nape of her neck looked sexy as hell. Her only jewelry was a gold necklace—no earrings.

Madi was everything he liked in a woman. Soft, sweet, smart. But he could also tell just by looking at her that she was the kind of woman who deserved the whole package—white picket fence, diamond ring, promises of forever. A partner who could protect her and love her unconditionally—without baggage.

She was someone's keeper.

But not his.

Yet, sitting there with her he...*ached*. Ached and yearned for more with her.

To hold *this* woman and lose himself in her.

Which was ridiculous. This was all fake. He knew it. Hell, he'd agreed to it.

So, why was he so tempted to break all the rules now?

Before he could contemplate that too much, Judith tapped Madi on the shoulder, interrupting them.

"I'm sorry," she said. "But could I have a moment, Madi?"

"Sure." Madi excused herself, then joined her boss in the foyer.

The auction moved ahead at full steam without her, people jumping up and waving as they bid. Telling himself he needed to stretch his aching leg and wasn't being nosy, Tate followed the two women. He lurked in the entranceway as he listened to their conversation.

"Absolutely," Madi said. "I'll go upstairs and get it right now. Thank you for the addition."

Then they parted ways.

Let it go, man. Let her go.

Tate knew he should go back inside and wait for her at the table. That would be the logical, sensible thing to do. They could finish out a nice night and then be done with it. Madi wasn't for him.

Except she was clearly under a lot of pressure here and she was still doing her best to keep everyone happy and supported. He felt that to his soul. He admired her for it, maybe because he'd done the same so many times himself.

Part of him screamed for him to walk away. Madi deserved *way* more than he could offer.

But the other part of him—the one that had been lonely too long—won out, and he followed her down the hall anyway.

Madi walked up the stairs, cursing the shoes pinching her toes as she searched for the antique Judith had so graciously donated to try and raise even more money for the clinic tonight.

Judith's family had built this theater in the early 1940s and apparently the "missing" vase had sat in the entry for years, until last spring when the theater had been renovated. It had never been put back on display and was worth several thousand dollars at least. Now all Madi had to do was find it.

The second story ran the length of the building. On one side was a series of rooms used by the rec center and various groups like the local Booster Club. On the other was one big closed-off storage area. Madi let herself in and flipped on the lights. Far above was an open-beam ceiling and a loft where more stuff had been haphazardly shoved away. Hopefully, she wouldn't have to climb up there in her dress and heels.

Warm and stuffy, the place smelled like neglect. She took a good look around and panicked at the idea of finding her way out of this maze, much less locating her quarry. She walked around a shelving unit stuffed to the gills with play props and background sets.

Past two huge fake potted Christmas trees. Large stacks of boxes. Madi kept searching. Near the center of the room were more containers of office equipment and furnishings, and miraculously, all by itself in the corner, a tall vase exactly like the one Judith had described. She grabbed it and turned to go, only to run into a brick wall of man.

Startled, she screamed and jumped back. The vase flew from her hands and would've smashed to the floor except Tate caught it and grinned. His dimples made him look boyish, except Tate Griffin was one hundred percent man.

"What are you doing?" Madi pressed a hand to her pounding heart. "You scared me half to death."

"Sorry." He winced slightly. "Anything I can help with?"

She snatched the vase from him. "No. This was all I needed."

He opened his mouth to say more, but the storage room door creaked open again and a voice called from somewhere far behind them, "Madi, dear? Are you in here?"

Oh, no. No, no, no.

This was not good. If Lucille found them in here, it would be all over social media by morning. She wanted to keep the town's focus on the auction, not her personal life. She glanced around for a place to hide.

Tate seemed to be on the same page because he held a finger to his lips, then took the vase in one hand and her wrist in the other to tug them into the shadows. Madi walked on tiptoe to avoid her heels clicking on the floor as they weaved through the shelves, his big body beside her, his breath in her ear. Stealth. Got it. Got something else too, an unexpected zing of wildfire through her blood as he leaned in to whisper, "She's persistent, isn't she?"

Madi nodded, biting her lip to keep from laughing.

Lucille called out for her again.

Scanning the area around them, Tate opened

an electrical panel and the next second the lights went out. Madi gasped as Tate pressed her into the wall, his lips on her cheek. "Don't move."

Then he crouched before her and removed her shoes one by one. Madi grasped his shoulders for balance, unable to see a thing. Tate, however, didn't seem to have that problem as he led her through a maze of more storage shelves with apparent ease. They turned corners and squeezed into spots, his hands sliding to her hips, guiding her where he wanted her to go, taking care she didn't bump into anything. She had no idea where they were headed now, but she followed him anyway, trusting him for some reason she didn't really understand. Then there was the fact that each time they stopped, he pressed against her again until she began to anticipate it. Crave it.

"Madi?" A small beam of light now accompanied Lucille's call. She had a flashlight.

"Oh, for the love of—" she started before Tate's warm lips silenced her. Her knees melted then, and if he hadn't been holding her up, she would've fallen. That's why she put her hand around his neck. For balance. Yep. That's the excuse she was going with anyway.

"How badly do you want to hide from her?" Tate asked when he finally pulled back a few millimeters, each word rumbling from his chest through hers. He'd set the vase on the floor beside them now, freeing up both hands to stroke her arms, her hair, cup her face. Madi rocked into him, unable to help herself, tightening her grip, her kiss-frazzled brain struggling to process words. It had been so long, too long since someone had touched her like this.

"Madi?" Tate whispered; his own voice laced with need.

She liked how he said her name. Liked how he made her feel too, languid yet throbbing. "Hmm?"

When she didn't continue, he huffed a small laugh against her jaw, then spun Madi away, nudging her up a nearby ladder, his biceps on either side of her arms, his chest pressed to her back. "Climb."

Good thing it was dark because her face felt hotter than the sun. Madi did as he asked, aware her butt was in his face as they went. And if he *could* see, then Tate had a great view right up her dress. Thankfully, she'd worn new lacy underwear tonight, but still. Not her best angle.

They reached the loft at the top of the ladder. Moonlight slanted in from a sole round window, revealing more stored items, a couch and a large table stacked with more stuff. There were also rows of framed pictures and empty planters. Everywhere.

Madi moved aside, but the space was so small she lost her balance and fell onto the couch.

Tate followed her down.

On the night of the storm, Madi had been beneath him too, but this time felt different. Sexy different.

He shifted a little to get the bulk of his weight off her. One of his thighs pushed between hers, and an involuntary, accidental moan escaped her, needy and wanton.

And horrifyingly loud.

They both stilled, peering down at the little beam of light as Lucille weaved through the aisles below.

"Unless she can climb a ladder, we're good here until she gives up and leaves," Tate whispered.

Yes. They were good here. Or very bad, depending on how you looked at it.

He went still, a solid heated package of testosterone and sinew pressing her into the sofa cushions. She felt a little helpless and every time he breathed, his leg shifted against her, sending shimmers of need through her whole body.

"She won't give up," Madi whispered back, more than a little breathless.

Tate pulled a coin from his pocket, then threw it. It landed with a ping all the way across the huge storage near the entrance.

"Oh!" Lucille's beam whipped toward the noise. "There you are!"

They watched as the older woman wobbled through the room to the door, then vanished.

Silence reigned, except for Madi's thundering pulse. She was in an attic loft, with her fake date.

Common sense screamed for her to leave. But her heart wanted him, just once.

"Okay?" Tate asked.

Loaded question. "You have some impressive skills, Mr. Griffin. I feel like a Bond girl."

His smile made her toes curl. "The way you shimmied up that ladder will fuel my fantasies for some time."

So he *could* see in the dark. And now that they were here, with bright moonlight streaming over them from the window, she saw him too. Felt him. *All* of him. He dropped his head, his lips barely brushing her exposed skin, and she sucked in a breath.

"I have lots of practice," she said for lack of anything better.

"Yeah?" he asked, sounding intrigued. "I haven't seen a lot of ladders in the ER."

"Oh, uh, no." Nerves had her laughing. And babbling. "But I cleared the gutters on my house last fall and nearly fell when I found a fist-sized spider waiting for me. Luckily, I managed not to accidentally break my neck."

Another chuckle escaped him.

"And thanks, by the way. For saving me." *Again.*

He slid a hand down her arm, squeezing her hip before cupping her butt. "My pleasure."

Her body liquefied at his touch, making her want to squirm closer to him. She felt things she hadn't in far too long and intended to go with those feelings.

"Hey." His low, sexy tone held a warning.

She'd wanted another kiss and more. She wriggled, hoping he got her message. "Yeah?"

"Are you coming on to me?"

"Well, technically, you're on top, so… I think that means *you're* coming on to *me*."

He pressed his forehead to hers and swore beneath his breath. Not the good kind of swear either.

Horrified and humiliated that he didn't want her after all, Madi pushed at him. "Sorry. I got caught up in the moment. I'm not very good at this, obviously. Excuse me."

"Not good at what, exactly?" Tate asked, loosening his hold on her so they could both sit up.

She sighed. "Men."

Tate looked over at her. "What's happening here?"

He was giving her an out, putting the power back in her hands. She appreciated it and somehow it made her want him even more. She wasn't sure of a lot of things at that moment, like how she'd deal with the fallout of all this tomorrow, but tonight, she was sure of one thing. She twined her fingers around his neck once more, leaning in to kiss him. "I want you, Tate."

He groaned low and deepened the kiss.

Things went a little crazy after that. His mouth

firm and hungry, his tongue sliding against hers.
Madi had almost forgotten what it was like to be
kissed like this, like there was nothing on earth
more important than her. The thrill of feeling soft
and feminine rushed over her. She'd experienced
it a few times in her sporadic dating life, but nothing like this. Nothing like this overwhelming need
for another person, like she'd die without having
him. This felt new and intoxicating. Inevitable.

Then Tate lifted his head. She touched his face,
the stubble on his jaw scraping against her fingers.
"To be clear, this is still just a fake date, right?"

"Right."

Then Tate's mouth was on hers again, and while
alarm bells went off deep inside Madi's brain, she
was tired of thinking, couldn't think anymore because man, Tate was good at this too. Even better
than his charm and flirting. She lost herself in his
lovemaking, how he didn't seem to be in a hurry
at all, like kissing her was an act all unto itself.
She panted for air when they finally broke apart,
Tate shifting to pull away, and Madi reflexively
clutched at him. "Wait—we're stopping?"

Dropping his head, his jaw rubbed hers. "Yeah."

"Why?"

He let out a low groan. "Because you're not
the one-night-stand-in-a-storage-room type of
woman."

Well, when he put it like that…

She always put other people's wants and needs

ahead of her own. But now, here, maybe she could have this just for herself. Besides, while she didn't know Tate well, she trusted him. He worked at the hospital. He was a medical professional like her. She knew he was polite and kind, and he'd spent time in Louisiana growing up. She knew he'd stepped in when she'd needed him, both as her date and with the auction, bidding on that expensive trip to Boston. And he'd just given her the most amazing kiss of her life. Maybe Tate Griffin wasn't her forever person, but he sure fit the bill for tonight.

"C'mon," she said, wrapping herself around him. "Please?"

This won her another long look. She ground against him, trying to sway the game in her favor.

After a huffed breath, Tate said, "You're sure?"

"I'm sure." Madi closed her eyes as his mouth blazed a path over her throat and collarbone. "I'm very, very sure."

When he encountered the material of her dress, a quick tug had the straps sliding down her shoulders to her elbows, trapping her hands at her sides and baring her breasts all in one movement.

Tate growled his approval, then paid careful homage to her body until she writhed beneath him as he moved down her stomach, taking her dress with him.

"So soft," he murmured across her skin, his breath a warm caress. But there was nothing gentle about him pushing the hem of her skirt up to her waist. He looked down at her thong, then slid the tiny slip of lace to one side, exposing all her secrets to his hot gaze. Lowering his head, he used his lips and tongue on her until Madi cried out her release, her hands gripping his head as stars exploded behind her eyes.

Before she'd stopped shuddering, he'd shoved off his jacket, then unbuckled and unzipped his pants and put on a condom. The sight of him ready for her made her moan. As he slowly pushed inside her, Madi lost her breath. Tate gave her a moment to adjust to his size, then his mouth found hers again. It was wildly sensuous, and all she could do was dig her fingernails into his back and hold on.

He swallowed her cries as he thrust, running a hand beneath her knee, lifting her leg up to wrap around his waist so he could go even deeper. Tate took her right out of herself, and Madi thrilled to it. He was powerful and primal, and she was there with him, meeting him halfway, unable to do anything but feel as he pushed her over the edge again. She was deep into another climax when he joined her, shuddering in her arms, his fingers digging into her hips as he lost himself in his pleasure.

Finally, tearing his mouth from hers, Tate dropped his head into the crook of Madi's neck, his shoulders rising and falling beneath her hands as he caught his breath and lifted his head to see her face.

"What?" she whispered.

"You're smiling."

Yes, she was. And probably would be for days. She'd just done something selfish, completely against her usual good-girl persona. She'd had sex. In a storage room. And it felt fantastic. Madi ran a finger over the bandage on his forehead, then along the bruise on his cheek. "I'm sorry you got hurt in the storm."

He shook his head, grinning. "I'm good."

They lay there like that for several long moments until thunderous applause rose in the distance, reminding Madi of where they were. Reluctantly, she nudged Tate, but he didn't move. "We need to go. Hurry. You first."

"I'm not leaving you up here," he said.

"Yes, you are. We can't be seen together." She pushed him again. "Go. Before Lucille comes back."

Not hurrying at all, Tate looked at her for another long moment, then pressed his lips to her damp temple and finally pulled away. He helped Madi straighten her clothing before taking care of himself.

Once he disappeared down the ladder again, Madi sat there alone, sated and introspective. Tate had given her exactly what she'd wanted tonight on all counts, fulfilling her fantasies and breaking

her out of her self-imposed mold for a little while.
They'd agreed to keep it simple. Just a fake date.
   And now it was over.

CHAPTER SEVEN

TATE SLEPT HARD that night and didn't dream. His morning went pretty much status quo. Mark met him on the beach, and they swam several miles before Tate went home to get ready for his shift. Because they were shorthanded, Tate also filled in on regular ambulance runs when needed, like today.

The shift was mainly of the normal variety. Chest pain call from Sunny Village Retirement Home that turned out to be gas. A kid who'd broken his arm during sports practice. Concussion on a construction site when a bucket of debris fell off a second-story roof and hit someone on the ground. Thank goodness for hard hats.

Then there was the baby. A five-month-old infant who needed flight transport to Wyckford General from a rural farming community due to a possible RSV infection. Since the local hospital was also a designated children's trauma center, they got a lot of transfers from other area hospitals for cases that were too much for the smaller places to handle. Normally, these runs weren't a problem for Tate. He kept focused on the job and blocked out everything else. But this patient was so small, he could hold her tiny body basically in one hand, and the bed in the chopper all but swallowed her whole.

The pilot, Rita, worked the controls while Tate stayed in the back of the chopper. The mom was quiet, her eyes never leaving her daughter as they hurried toward Wyckford General. The father drove himself in the family SUV. From what Tate had gathered at the scene, the couple had moved to the US from Somalia a few years back, fleeing war and starvation and looking for a better life. He hoped they'd find one and that their baby girl would live to see it.

Respiratory syncytial virus, RSV, was a common contagion that normally caused either basic cold or flu-like symptoms and generally people recovered within a few days. But this baby girl also had an underlying heart problem and her case had turned severe, her condition deteriorating rapidly and requiring flight transport.

Luckily, since they'd picked her up, the baby's blood pressure had improved and her O2 sats were at eighty-nine to ninety, which was an improvement. Tate kept a close eye on all the monitors and IVs hooked up to their tiny patient as Rita landed on the helipad atop the hospital, then came around to help Tate get the patient and her mother out of the back.

Brock was there to meet them. He also pulled shifts in the ER when he wasn't holding office hours or home with his fiancée and daughter. Honestly, Tate wasn't sure how the man did it. But Brock looked happier than Tate had ever seen him, even though he was worked to death, so the man was obviously doing something right these days.

"What have we got?" Brock asked as they wheeled the tiny patient into the hospital and onto an elevator headed down to the first floor.

Tate gave him the rundown on the baby's stats and condition on the way, telling him about the case. As they reached their destination and rushed their tiny patient toward an open trauma bay, Tate helped lift the infant girl from the gurney to the bed. "She's currently got an open port in her left femoral for medications, if needed, and a PIV in her right hand. There were some ST elevations during transport that were concerning."

"Okay," Brock said, already moving, checking the baby's vitals and neurological responses. "Team, let's have some epi, just in case, and a resus cart if she codes."

Tate stepped back to let the ER team take over, noticing Madi there too. She caught his eyes and held a moment before looking away and concentrating on their new little patient. He got it. When you worked under emergency conditions you had to be at the top of your game and keep your focus where it belonged because things changed in an instant and you didn't get a second chance. Tate knew that all too well.

But this patient was safe, for now, and in the best possible hands, so he could step back and take note. Every movement Madi made was part of a well-choreographed routine the analytical part of him appreciated and admired. Almost as much as he'd admired how she'd felt in his arms last night.

Whoops. Nope. Not going there, dude.

"Her blood pressure's falling," Madi said, jarring Tate out of his thoughts. "Sixty-six over fifty-three. End-tidal CO_2 is seventeen. Heart rate's one hundred and nine. O2 sats at eighty-eight."

"Get her on a ventilator," Brock said. "And get cardiology down here stat."

Madi assisted with intubating the tiny patient to help her breathe.

Tate and Rita were free to go, but he couldn't seem to tear himself away from the scene just yet. He needed to know the baby would be okay. And he liked watching Madi work. Maybe a bit too much.

"Since we're taking a break," Rita said, "I'm gonna go call Maureen. She's been texting me all morning about the kids' softball lessons. Be back in a few."

Tate hiked his chin in acknowledgment, his gaze still locked on the medical scene before him. "Tell your wife I said hi."

"Will do," Rita said as she walked away.

Brock glanced at the patient's chart on the large wall monitor. "She's stable for now. Looks like the patient is on dopamine, ketamine and fentanyl. Possible hypoxic heart event on the ride over here..."

"How is my daughter?" a voice asked from behind Tate.

He turned to find the mother and father in the hall behind him. After a final glance into the trauma bay, Tate led them down to a private waiting area, out of the hustle and bustle of the ER. He didn't have kids of his own, but serving in conflicts around the world and talking to survivors of horrific ordeals, he knew how to comfort people. Even if those skills didn't extend to himself.

They sat down, the mother and father on one side of the small room, and Tate in a chair across from them, as he explained what was happening with their infant daughter. "She's not in any pain. Her condition is the same as when we left the other hospital earlier."

"Will you be here with us?" the father asked him.

"I'll be going back on my shift as soon as my partner gets back. We're paramedics. We go out to the scene and bring patients into the doctors and nurses here who'll care for them."

"Oh." The mother looked disappointed. "I thought you were the doctor."

"No. I'm a first responder. An emergency medical technician. I'm also in the military, Air Force Pararescue. I'm home on extended leave right now." He left out the rest of story because they didn't need to know about the accident, about his failure. "And I'm glad I was here to help your daughter today. I know what it's like to be on the other side of things."

"Thank you." The father shook Tate's hand. "You did a very good job."

After that, Tate went back upstairs to check on Rita and the chopper. His leg bothered him a bit, but he ignored it. He deserved the pain, to remind himself of his guilt, instead of thinking about Madi and how sweet and warm and giving she'd been in that loft.

She'd been…*amazing*, revving his engine good. Every time he thought about how she'd looked spread out for him on that couch, his body reacted.

Which was stupid.

Yes, last night with Madi had been great. But that's as far as it went. They'd agreed.

He hadn't acted honorably when he'd slept with her, but he could now.

The less contact they had going forward the better. It was a one-night stand. Time to move on.

The rest of the day went smoothly with no major issues.

He checked in on the infant patient after their final run of the shift, and she was holding steady, which was about the best they could hope for at that point.

By the time Tate got home that evening, he took a long, hot shower, then pulled on clean clothes while eyeballing the empty Vicodin bottle on his dresser. This was his ritual, the stare-down. In the end, he shoved the thing into his pocket like he always did, wanting the reminder to keep his head on straight.

Then he drove the Chevelle into town for dinner. Wyckford was one of those storybook seaside towns where tourists flocked in the summer, and everything went quiet and still in the winter. Set on the rocky shores of Buzzards Bay, Wyckford offered a quirky, eclectic mix of old and new architecture. Victorian buildings painted in bright colors lined the main drag, housing the grocer, post office, gas station and hardware store. Farther down was a turnoff to the beach itself, where a long pier jutted into the water, with more shops, an arcade and Ferris wheel. Before you got there though, you got to the Buzzy Bird Café.

It was like something from the 1950s, all black-and-white tiled floors, red vinyl booths and chrome accents. Tate walked in, noting a new front door and windows had been installed since the storm. He took a seat at the lunch counter where his physical therapist poured him a mug of coffee. He'd had this same nightly routine for months. Luna didn't ask questions, and Tate really appreciated that.

Tonight, she dropped a tablet computer in front of him and cocked a hip.

Tate gave her a level look. Her expression had unhappy written all over it. She was dressed in a black shirt, black pants, black boots, all topped with a frilly pink apron with a cartoon buzzard on the front. She pointed toward the screen with a raised brow, and Tate finally read it.

Annual Hospital Auction Huge Success!

So far so good. Then he read the first paragraph, which credited it all to Madison Scott, who'd attended the event with her new boyfriend—Tate Griffin.

Boyfriend? Yikes. Still, it wasn't a big deal. Stuff like this blew over. When the next scandal hit, they'd be old news. He passed the tablet back to Luna and shrugged. "What's the special tonight?"

Luna crossed her arms. "The special is what's going on between you and my best friend?"

"Nothing," he said, unsure where this was going or why it was any of her business.

"Look. When I suggested she ask you to be her date, I figured it was a win-win situation. Madi gets a hot guy to parade around on her arm, and you get a fun night with no strings attached. But the title 'boyfriend' means something. How did that happen?"

"I don't know." He didn't like being put on the defensive here, especially because he kind of wondered the same thing himself. How had he let things go so far? And sure, Lucille was a gossipy old biddy who'd probably make up salacious stuff about the Pope if she thought it would increase her follower count but still. Tate had been raised by two parents familiar with the military. His dad had been gone a lot, serving as a pilot in the Air Force. And his mom had worked as a secretary at the Pentagon. And his job in pararescue had required knowledge, skill, discipline, the ability to think on your feet and be decisive and honorable.

The honorable part troubled him now.

Because despite being up-front about it all, he'd somehow managed to care about Madi and convinced himself that having sex with her last night was an easy fix for them both. She was lonely. He was lonely. But in hindsight, their choice was a bad one. Because while he'd move on to his next deployment someday soon, Madi lived here and had more at stake.

God, I'm such an idiot.

Luna continued to stare a hole in his head until he shrugged and said, "I won't hurt her. I promise."

The words tasted bitter on his tongue, probably because he knew they weren't true. Madi was an adult, yes, but even knowing just a little about her, he could see how good and softhearted she was.

No way she'd make it out of this unscathed. On the flip side, neither would he. Because despite his best intentions, Tate had let his emotions and his heart get involved where Madi was concerned.

As if reading his mind, Luna muttered something under her breath and walked away.

He ate dinner fast, then returned to his big, empty house to work in the garage some more. He'd seen the Chevelle in the newspaper right after he'd arrived and hadn't been able to resist her.

He'd never been able to resist a sweetheart of a car.

Or a sweetheart of a woman either, apparently...

The next day, Madi sat in a hospital board meeting surrounded by a bunch of administrators who included her boss and her mother. Her mind, however, was a million miles away. Or, more accurately, in the trauma bay where she'd seen Tate Griffin.

Obviously, they'd run into each other at work, but even so, she hadn't been prepared for him. It had taken everything she had not to go after him in the hall after he'd left with the infant's parents. Just to say hello. Just to—

Gah!

She had to forget about their night together. Forget the fact she'd never gone up in flames for a man so fast in her entire life. Then, yesterday, he hadn't even said a word to her. He'd obviously moved on. She should too. That'd teach her to have inappropriate sex with a man she worked with.

But all it had really taught Madi was that she'd been missing out. Worse, the magnitude of her attraction for Tate Griffin had her afraid the next time they crossed paths at work or anywhere else, she might shove him into the nearest closet for round two.

"Madison? The amount we raised?" Judith repeated.

"Uh, eighteen thousand." Madi looked down at the paper in front of her to be sure. "All of which will go toward the Health Services Clinic budget for the year."

"Unfortunately, we may have to make some adjustments going forward," Bud Lofton, head of the board and chief hospital administrator, said. Tall and fit, he looked younger than his fifty-five years. With sharp eyes and a sharper mind, he was all about the bottom line. He did listen though, which Madi appreciated.

"Adjustments?" She knew better than to show weakness. "But we need the money to support our programs. People rely on those services in this town."

"Be that as it may, we've encountered some unexpected financial constraints," Bud said, "that require us to take another look at the budget and where funds are allocated."

Madi glanced at the other board members to see their reactions. Brock looked rumpled and gorgeous as usual. His blue eyes warmed when he met her gaze. No one else made eye contact with her though, which meant they all probably knew this news already. Great.

"But the free clinic is more important than ever," Madi said. "Nowhere in this entire county provides drug addiction and teen pregnancy counseling or an abuse hotline. We give necessary health care to an underserved population."

The HSC was important to her, and not just because Karrie had died because she'd had no place to get the services she'd so desperately needed. Madi intended to make sure that no other scared eighteen-year-old girl felt the helplessness and terror her sister had.

"We understand the importance of the clinic's mission. But we must also balance that with what benefits the whole medical center. There won't be a clinic if the rest of the facility goes under, Madi."

"Our numbers are good, Bud. Within our budget," she said, needing his support. "Plus, we're eligible for grant programs and funding. And because we're located in the old west wing of the hospital, one hundred percent of any money we do bring in goes directly into the services we offer. Why is this even being discussed?"

"Because the full liability for the HSC is the hospital's as well," Bud said.

That was true, unfortunately. Madi tried again to appeal to Bud's fiscal side. "But we've run in the black for the last two years. We've never had an incident. We make sense for our community, Bud, and it's the right thing to do." She paused, then added, "And I'll continue to champion it until my dying breath."

He shook his head. "Madi, I admire your tenacity and your belief in the clinic's mission. I want to be on your side here. But let's look at the other aspect of it—the clinic also brings a certain demographic to Wyckford, and a portion of the town isn't really behind this." Bud sat quietly a moment. "But I'll make you a deal. At this week's town meeting we propose our budget for next year. I'll give everyone a formal spiel about the clinic and the challenges we face, then ask for public thoughts."

Madi stifled a groan. Everyone went to the town meetings in Wyckford. If Bud wanted opinions, he'd get them—in droves.

"If there's a positive response, the HSC continues as normal," Bud concluded. "If not, then we'll reevaluate. Acceptable?"

Since Madi didn't have much choice, all she could say was, "Yes, sir."

"Oh, one more thing. When did the clinic's budget include a pharmacy delivery service?"

Bud must be referring to Madi picking up Mr. Martin's meds that morning and bringing them to the old man's home. It wasn't a mystery how he'd found out. Wyckford had one pharmacy, located in the only grocery store, which everyone in town used often. Anyone could have seen her, and Madi hadn't made a secret of what she was doing.

She felt an eye twitch coming on, but she didn't let it deter her. "I did that on my own time, sir."

An hour later, Madi was back to work on the ER floor, thankful the meeting and a crazy shift had at least given her something to think about other than Tate. She hadn't seen him since yesterday and assumed he wasn't working. Or maybe he'd start after she was gone for the day. Either way she wouldn't ask because that would be too pathetic.

Instead, she concentrated on the many new cases coming in. A stroke victim, a diabetic with gangrene in his toes, a guy who'd been stabbed in a bar in Boston and made it all the way to Wyckford before deciding he should get treatment. Plus, two drunks, a stomachache and a bad case of poison ivy.

When she yawned for the tenth time, Madi went in search of coffee. As she stood in the break room, her mind wandered again to that storage room loft and Tate's warm hands, rough and gentle at the same time, stroking her—

"Honey?"

She blinked and the daydream faded, replaced by the sight of her mother.

"I called your name three times. What in the world are you thinking about today?"

Madi couldn't tell her mom her X-rated thoughts, so she said, "Dessert."

"Madi," her mother murmured, giving her a skeptical look. "This isn't like you. Allowing yourself to get distracted by a man."

"I'm not distracted," Madi said even as her face heated. "I've just got a lot on my plate right now."

"And that's different from any other time how?"

"Can you please just drop it? I'm fine, okay?" Madi said.

"Are you sure?" her mother asked.

"Yes. You're worrying about nothing."

A fellow nurse named Camilla, twenty-two and fresh out of school, ran in, all but quivering with excitement. "He's here. In the waiting room."

"Who's here?" Madi frowned.

Camilla gave her a pointed look. "Him."

"Does 'him' have a name?" her mother asked dryly.

"Tate Griffin. That hot flight paramedic!"

Her mother slid Madi a look, but she was too busy trying to keep her heart from pounding out of her chest. "Tate's here to see me?"

"No. He asked for Dr. Turner," Camilla said in a rush. "But Dr. Turner's been called away."

"I'll tell him." Madi headed down the hallway

toward the ER. At least her scrubs were stain-free, always a bonus. But she couldn't remember if she'd put on makeup that morning, and really wished she'd had time to brush her hair.

Tate sat in the waiting room, head back and eyes closed, one leg stretched out in front of him. Today he wore faded Levi's and a black T-shirt, looking like the poster boy for Tall, Dark and Mysterious. Anyone would assume he was asleep, but Madi sensed Tate was about as relaxed as a coiled rattler.

As she approached, he opened his eyes and looked at her but said nothing. His piercing green-gold gaze sent her nervous system haywire. She'd just handled three emergencies in a row without a blip, but now her blood raced like the Indy 500.

He didn't come here to see you. Act cool.

The air-conditioning blasted over her skin, which in no way explained why Madi felt like she was in the throes of a sudden hot flash as she stopped before him and bit her lower lip.

Tate rose from his chair and Madi's breath caught. Which wasn't good.

She needed to get a grip.

No one else was in the waiting room, for once, but just across the hall at the sign-in desk sat Camilla and her mother, neither pretending to do anything other than stare at them in open, rapt curiosity.

Madi ignored their audience as best she could. "You're here to see Brock?"

"Yeah. I need to get my stitches out. I'd do it myself but the angle's awkward, so…"

"I'll remove them for you," Madi blurted before she could think better of it. "Brock got called out."

Her mother and Camilla were still watching, now joined by additional staff who apparently had nothing better to do than eavesdrop. She'd lay odds this meeting would go public by the end of her shift, but there was nothing she could do about it now. "C'mon. Let's go."

She looked at Tate from beneath her lashes as they walked toward an open exam room in the ER—at his big, tough body, and the way he limped ever so slightly on his left leg. Then she hazarded another glance at his face and found him watching her too, looking bemused. She showed him into the room, then pulled the curtain. "I'll grab a kit and be right back."

CHAPTER EIGHT

IN THE AIR FORCE, Tate had learned defense tactics and ways to conceal information. He excelled at both. As a result, concealing emotion came all too easily to him. There wasn't much room for emotion in the high-stress, high-stakes world of emergency medicine. So, he'd long ago perfected the blank expression, honed it as a valuable tool. It was second nature now or had been.

Until Madi, it seemed.

Because he was having a hell of a hard time pulling it off with her. Like now, for instance, when he was relieved to see her again today and yet struggling to hide that very fact.

She was a great nurse. He'd seen it firsthand yesterday with the infant. Also, on the night of the storm, she'd been extremely levelheaded and composed. And she looked cute in her purple scrubs with the tiny red heart embroidered over the front pocket. He especially liked her air of authority.

Honestly, he liked everything about her so far, including how she'd tasted.

Tate didn't get to think about that long though

because someone moaned from the exam space next door, the sound laced with both fear and pain. He stood, reacting on instinct to the call to help.

The moan came again. He stuck his head around the curtain and saw a guy hooked up to a monitor, fluids and oxygen. He was maybe in his early fifties, smelled like a brewery even from several feet away and either hadn't showered this month or rolled in garbage. The man's gray hair stuck out all over, some missing in clumps. Homeless, by the looks of him. He seemed small and weak and terrified.

"You okay, buddy?" he asked, staying where he was. "You need a nurse?"

The man shook his head, eyes wide, his free hand flailing. His pupils were dilated, so he was probably high on something.

Cursing, Tate moved to the bedside and checked the IV. They were hydrating him, which was good. Catching the guy's hand in his, he squeezed lightly. "What's going on?"

"My stomach hurts."

The filthy sleeve of the man's shirt had torn away enough to reveal an eagle seal tattoo on his arm. Tate let out a slow breath, feeling raw. "You were in the military?"

"Army," the man slurred, clearly still heavily intoxicated.

Tate might have turned away then, but the guy

clung to his hand like it was a lifeline, so he slowly sat on a stool instead.

"I'm Air Force. Pararescue." Tate exhaled slow. "I'm on leave."

"You never leave," the man said.

True enough.

"They should pay us for the nightmares," the guy continued, his voice rougher now, like it took more effort to speak. "They should give us extra combat wages for all the ways they messed up our lives."

Silence settled, the man looking half asleep now, and Tate felt a little sick. In his gut. In the depths of his soul.

"I still think about them," the man whispered out of the blue.

Tate didn't have to ask who. All the dead. He swallowed hard and nodded.

The man stared at him, glassy-eyed but coherent. "How many for you?"

"Four." But there'd been others, too. *Way* too many others.

The man let out a shuddery sigh of sympathy, sliding a shaky hand into his shirt and coming out with a flask, which he held out to Tate. "Here. This helps."

Madi chose that moment to return, pulling back the curtain. "*There* you are," she said to Tate, then smiled kindly at the man in the bed. "Better yet, Mr. Ryan?"

Mr. Ryan didn't meet her gaze as he gave a jerky nod.

"Why don't I hold that for you, okay?" Gently, she pried the flask from his fingers.

Tate didn't know what he'd expected from her. Maybe annoyance—or resentment for having to care for a guy whose wounds were clearly self-inflicted ones. But instead, she ran a hand down the old vet's arm in a comforting gesture, not shying away from touching him.

More than duty. Much more.

"I've called your daughter," she told the man. "She'll be here in ten minutes. We'll let the IV do its thing, refilling you with minerals, potassium, sodium and other good stuff. You'll feel better soon." She patted his forearm over the tattoo, then checked his lead before gesturing to Tate to follow her.

"Is he okay?" he asked quietly on the other side of the curtain.

"He will be once he sobers up."

"I could tell from his eyes he's on something besides alcohol."

"Yes."

"Does he have a place to stay?"

She gave him a pointed stare. "Look at you with all the questions."

"Does he?"

She sighed. "I'm sorry, but I can't discuss his

case with you. I can tell you he's taken care of. Does that help?"

Tate had no idea what the lump in his throat was doing or why his heart hurt. Or why he couldn't let this go. "He's a veteran. He's having nightmares. He—"

"I know." She touched him too, soothing him as she had Mr. Ryan. "And like I said, he's being cared for." Madi paused then, studying Tate for a disturbingly long beat. "Not everyone would have gone in there and comforted him."

"I'm not everyone."

The phone at her hip vibrated. She looked at the screen and let out a breath. "Sorry. Sit tight for me for a few minutes. I'll be right back."

Then she strode off again.

In the exam space on the other side of Tate was another patient. The curtain between them was shut too, but it suddenly whipped open as another nurse talked to the patient in the bed. "Change into the robe. I'll go page your doctor."

This guy had clearly walked in under his own steam but wasn't looking good. Big, midthirties, dressed in coveralls with the Wyckford Public Utilities Department logo on the front. He was filthy from head to toe, clearly just off the job. As Tate watched, the man went from looking bad to worse. Then he gasped, clutching at his chest.

Christ.

Tate hurtled back in time to the open ocean,

squinting against the brilliant fireball of wreckage. He'd clung to a piece of floating door, praying help would arrive in time…

Now, a million miles away and four years later, the guy in the next hospital bed groaned, dropping his gown as he slithered to the floor, his eyes rolling up in his head.

Tate yelled, "He's coding!"

And the dance to save the man's life began. Madi rushed in, assisting Tate with CPR, checking the patient's vitals and finally shocking him with a defibrillator to get his heart started again when all else failed. It went on for maybe five minutes but felt like a lifetime. Finally, they had the patient stabilized and a cardiologist took over. Madi led Tate back to his exam space and shut the curtain, a suture removal kit in her hand.

She gave him a sharp look. "Thanks for your help there."

He didn't respond. Didn't move.

So she pointed to the bed and said with soft steel in her voice, "Sit."

He did, but on the stool. The bed was for patients, and Tate wasn't a patient. Not really.

Madi washed her hands thoroughly, then pulled on gloves and opened the kit she'd brought. She stood in front of him and carefully removed his bandage, yawning.

He smiled. "Tired?"

"I passed tired three hours ago." She soaked a

gauze pad in rubbing alcohol and cleaned the area around his sutures, then picked up a pair of tweezers. "Don't worry. I'm an expert at getting these out quickly and relatively painlessly."

He wrapped his fingers around her wrist, stopping her. "Why are your cheeks flushed?"

She hesitated, then finally admitted, "I'm embarrassed, okay?"

This stopped him cold. "About what?"

"What do you think?" She looked confused. "What happened the other night."

"Why?"

She sighed, her warm minty breath tickling the hair near his temple. He suppressed a shiver of awareness.

"Because I'd never done the whole casual sex thing." She lowered her voice to a soft whisper. "And now…" Her eyes slowly met his. "I'm thinking I should have requested a two-night stand."

Her candor left Tate speechless.

Madi winced and shook her head, then laughed as she leaned in close to examine his stitches. "Brock does nice work. But you'll probably still have a scar. Shouldn't be too much of a problem for you though. Women like that. Fall all over themselves."

Except he wasn't looking for a woman. He wasn't looking for anything.

Right?

Madi used the tweezers to pull up a stitch,

then snipped it with scissors. "A little sting," she warned, then pulled it out. "Do you like being a paramedic?"

He shrugged.

Madison continued working, her gaze steady on him. She had great eyes. Warm brown and sparkling with humor and intelligence.

The nurse from the front desk he'd talked to when he came in poked her head around the curtain, her eyes on Tate as she asked, "Need any help?"

"Nope." Madi kept working. "I've got this, Camilla."

The woman's face fell, and she left without further comment.

Two seconds later Madi's mother appeared. She waved to Tate, then yanked the curtain shut again, leaving them alone once more.

"Your mom's nice," Tate said.

"Yep." Madi pulled another stitch, and he barely felt it. She was right. She was good at this.

He stared at her, truly fascinated in a way that surprised him. Madi was supposed to be just a cute nurse in a small town he'd soon forget.

Except…he wasn't forgetting her. Not at all.

"Hey, Madi." Yet another woman peeked around the curtain, this one wearing a housekeeping outfit. "Need anything?"

"No," Madi snapped.

"Fine," the woman said, clearly insulted. "You don't have to take my head off."

When she vanished, Madi took a deep breath and turned away to dump her used instruments into the sink. "That was my sister. Toni. What about your leg?"

Tate scowled. "What about it?"

She looked at him over her shoulder with an expectant air, saying nothing. It made him smile. She said, "You can't use that silence thing against me. I invented it."

"What silence thing?"

She shook her head. "Some secrets are toxic if you try to keep them inside. They eat you up. You aren't married, are you?"

"No."

"Attached? Have a girlfriend? Or boyfriend?"

"No." Tate waved her questions away, changing subjects as she pulled off her gloves and tossed them in the biohazard bin. "Does your whole family work here?"

"Just my mom, my sister and me," she said. "And I also run the Health Services Clinic."

"Is there a need in a town this small?" Tate ran a finger over his now stitch-free cut.

"A huge one. We have a high teenage pregnancy rate, and drug abuse is on the rise everywhere. So is homelessness. Counseling services and advocacy and educational programs are vital. And we have weekly free office hours for those who can't afford medical care."

She sounded so fierce his heart ached all over again. He'd once had that same fire. Hopefully she'd never lose her genuine compassion to jaded cynicism like him. "What made you take on all that extra work?"

Madi cleaned up the counter. "Someone had to."

"Ah," he said. "You're one of those."

"One of those what?" She glanced at him, eyes narrowed. "Look. How about we make a deal? I'll answer one of your questions for every one of mine you answer for me."

He knew better than to go there. By all appearances, she was pretty and sweet and innocent, but beneath that guileless smile, Madison Scott held all the power, and Tate knew it. She'd have him confessing his sins with one warm touch.

When he didn't respond, she shook her head. "Figured that'd be too much for you."

It was. Tate should leave…but he opened his mouth anyway. "What time are you off?"

From the surprised look she gave him, he'd shocked her. Fair enough. He'd shocked himself too.

"Seven," Madi said. "Why?"

"I'll pick you up."

"For what?"

"A date."

She seemed to consider that a second, then said, "No. You know the pier?"

"Sure. Isn't it closed this time of year?"

"Some things are still open. I'll meet you there. In front of the Ferris wheel."

"Okay. I'll be there."

CHAPTER NINE

As MADI GOT into her car after her shift, her phone rang.

"Tate came to the hospital to see you?" Luna asked.

Madi didn't bother to ask how she knew. Honestly, she wouldn't have been surprised to see it as the leading headline in the paper. "Yes, he did. I'm meeting him in about fifteen minutes. Any words of advice?"

"Just be careful. Make sure you're both on the same page."

"I will," Madi said. "I need to go."

When she got to the pier, Madi took a moment to inhale the crisp, sea air while the sound of waves lapping the shore soothed her antsy nerves. Flyers were posted for an upcoming event at the local high school—a play the following week— and another for the town's monthly Interested Citizens Meeting where Bud Lofton would share the hospital's budget.

Her stress levels rose again, but she didn't have time to dwell on it. She had other things to think about now. She'd changed out of her scrubs before she'd left work, into jeans and a cute, pink sweater that brought out the copper highlights in her brown hair.

As she walked to the now dormant Ferris wheel, Madi checked her reflection in the back window of a closed food truck. The night was chilly, and the power of the water rocking gently against the pylons far below made the pier shudder faintly with the push and pull of the tide, matching the anticipation drumming through her.

You're not going to sleep with him again. It was a one-time thing. You're only here because you're curious.

Curious, yes. But also, she had a problem. A big, moth-to-a-flame type of attraction. Why? Madi had no idea. Their goodbye in the loft on the night of the auction had been…abrupt. But everything before then had been…*amazing*.

She stopped just past the Ferris wheel, and the hair at the back of her neck prickled. Madi turned to find Tate watching her as he leaned back against the pier railing, his long legs casually crossed at the ankles, looking for all the world like a guy who made a habit of hanging out on piers and strolling lazy beaches.

They both knew that wasn't true.

And man, he looked good. Stubble darkened his jaw, and his firm, sensuous mouth held a faint hint of a smile. The new scar above his brow was still shiny and only added to his whole ruffian look. He'd changed from earlier too, into dark jeans and a black sweatshirt with the Air Force insignia across his broad chest. He looked bad and built and dangerous as hell.

And he was hers for the evening.

Mine.

And Tate Griffin made Madi feel. A lot. Curious, annoyed, frustrated and—aroused.

That last one topped the list presently. She wanted to lick him head to toes.

His green-gold gaze held steady. Madi couldn't guess what he was thinking, but she flushed a little anyway for where her own thoughts had gone. Right into the smutty pool.

He pushed away from the railing and strode toward her, the slight limp only making him sexier and more intriguing. When he got to her, Tate took her hand and pulled her around to the side of the pier, out of view, between two storage sheds.

"W-what are you doing?" she asked.

Instead of answering, he lifted her up on her tiptoes and kissed her.

Madi slid her fingers into his hair. And when his tongue touched hers again, all her bones melted away. Then, before she knew it, it was over and she was back on her feet, weaving unsteadily as she blinked him into focus. "What was *that*?"

Tate shrugged. "Sorry. Been thinking about that since earlier. You're distracting."

"And you're not?"

His eyes heated. "We could fix that."

"Oh, no." She stepped back. "You said you weren't a long-term bet. Not even a short one."

He pressed her into the railing and kissed her again. Apparently, discussion time was over. Which was okay because Madi couldn't form words when he touched her like this. His tongue in her mouth, her hands cupping his head, their bodies mashed together. She'd have climbed him like a tree if she could. Then his muscled thigh slid between hers. He felt so...*good*.

Then, drawing on some reserve of strength she didn't know she had, Madi pushed away. For a beat Tate didn't budge, then he moved back slowly, his eyes heavy lidded and his lips parted.

"Okay," she said shakily. "Let's try something that's *not* going to lead to round two of sex in a public place. Talking. Were you in the military?"

Besides the sweatshirt, she'd noticed how he carried himself. Calm, steady, ready for anything. Then there was his bone-deep stoicism. And the way he'd interacted with the old, homeless vet Mr. Ryan—like he knew to the depths of his soul what the other man had felt.

"I still am. Addicted to the adrenaline rush," Tate said, then crossed his arms as he leaned his hips back against the railing. "Now it's my turn. Why me?"

"Why you what?" Madi squirmed a little under

his scrutiny. They both knew what he was asking and playing coy didn't do her any favors. He already knew that what they'd done that night at the auction had been a first for her because she'd told him as much, but what he didn't know, *couldn't* know, was that she'd only been able to do it with him at all because she'd felt something for him. She shrugged too. "Like I said, it'd been a long time."

"But you don't sleep around."

It wasn't a question.

"No. I felt…connected to you," she admitted.

He looked serious now as he slowly shook his head. "You don't want to feel connected to me."

"I can't help it. And there's more."

"You used me to chase away your restlessness," he said quietly.

"Yes." Madi winced, not sure how he knew, but it wasn't really a well-kept secret that she had no life, so… "I'm sorry."

"Don't be. You can use me any time."

"But we agreed it was only a one-time thing," she reminded him, her throat suddenly very dry. "I think I need a drink."

Tate smiled but didn't challenge her. They walked toward the arcade down the way. He watched her, his look hot and dark, causing another of those tingles inside her to start up again.

"Back to our question game," she said to distract herself. "Are you going back to the Air Force when your leave is over?"

"Yes." His eyes stayed on her lips. She was playing with fire, and she knew it.

"You know this whole man of mystery thing isn't as cute as you might think," she said.

"I'm not trying to be cute." A smile curved his mouth as he seemed to come to a decision. "You already know everything you need to about me, Madi. I'm in the military. I'm a thrill seeker. I'm on leave. Eventually I'll go back. Small-town life isn't really for me."

"I doubt that's everything about you." She eyed him skeptically. "How'd you hurt your leg?"

"An accident."

He hadn't hesitated to say it, but Madi sensed his big-time reluctance to talk about it further.

"I'm sorry." She didn't want to push, knowing exactly how it felt to *not* want to discuss something painful, but she wished he'd say more about himself. She was curious, that's all. "What brought you to Wyckford?"

"Mark Bates told me about it. He said he thought it would be a good place to relax and recoup."

"And is it?" she asked softly.

"It has its moments."

Madi fought the ridiculous urge to hug him but stopped herself. They didn't know each other well but she wasn't sure Tate would welcome it just then. "From the limp I'd guess your leg still bothers you. Are you taking anything for it?"

"No." He placed his hand at the small of her back and steered her into the indoor arcade. Conversation over, apparently. Tate gave the guy behind the Shooting Duck Gallery some money, then picked up one of the toy guns like he knew what he was doing and sighted and shot, hitting every duck and destroying the entire row.

"Show-off." Madi tried it herself, but she didn't know what she was doing and didn't hit a single thing. She sighed.

"Pathetic. Pick up the gun again." Tate handed over more cash, then stood behind her, correcting her stance by nudging his foot between hers to move her legs farther apart. Then he steadied her arms with his own, practically wrapping himself around her, surrounding her. If she turned her head, she could kiss his rock-solid bicep. And it shocked her how much she wanted to do just that. Madi bet he'd taste better than any drink she could order.

Tate went still, then let out a low breath, the side of his face brushing her jaw. "I know what you're thinking."

Madi hoped not. Then he pressed more firmly against her, and yep—he knew. Her face heated, and her throat constricted.

"Shoot the ducks, Madison," he growled.

With him guiding her, she hit one, and her competitive nature kicked in.

"Again," she demanded.

With a grin, Tate slapped more money onto the counter.

"Show me what you've got." He stepped back this time, leaving her to do it alone.

She took out one from the entire row. So annoying. "How do you make it look so easy?"

"Practice." His tone said he'd had lots. "Your concentration needs work."

Her concentration wasn't the problem. She was just focused on the wrong things. Like how his arms felt around her, how his hard body had been pressed to her back. Awareness shimmered through her bloodstream. Far too much for her liking. "Maybe I don't care about being able to shoot a duck."

"Then don't." He tossed down another few bucks and obliterated another row of ducks himself.

"Dude." The guy behind the counter looked impressed as he presented Tate with a huge teddy bear.

"Thanks," Madi said as Tate handed her the prize. She hugged the bear close, the silly gesture giving her warm fuzzies. Which was ironic because nothing about Tate Griffin should have given Madi warm fuzzies.

He clearly didn't want to be her hero.

They went to the squirt gun booth next, where Tate proceeded to soundly beat Madi three times in a row. Apparently, he wasn't worried about her ego either. He won a stuffed dog, then laughed out loud as Madi attempted to carry both animals and navigate the aisles without bumping into anyone.

It was ridiculous. *She* was ridiculous. Because no way would she fall for a guy just because he won her silly stuff she didn't need.

You're not supposed to fall for him at all…

They competed in a driving game next, side by side, fighting for first place. Tate handled his steering wheel with easy concentration, paying Madi no attention whatsoever. But she was too busy watching him out of the corner of her eye and fell behind as a result. Tate grinned, which meant he was paying attention to her.

Just to make sure, she nudged him with her shoulder.

His grin widened, but he didn't take his eyes off the game. "Won't work. You're going down."

Never one to turn down a challenge, Madi let her breast brush his arm.

"Playing dirty," he warned, voice low, both husky and amused.

But she absolutely had his attention. She did the boob thing again, her eyes on the screen, so she didn't notice when he leaned closer. Then he nipped her earlobe, soothing the tiny ache with his tongue. That's all it took. Her knees wobbled and her foot slipped off the gas.

Her car crashed into the wall while Tate sped across the finish line.

"Cheater!" she complained. "You can't—"

Tate kissed her until she couldn't remember what she'd been saying. When he pulled away finally, Madi rested against the booth because her legs felt like jelly.

"You started it." Tate kissed before taking her hand and leading her over to the snack bar in the arcade. He bought them both dinner, and she and Tate—with the two huge stuffed animals—sat there to eat.

"You're doing PT for your leg, right?" she asked, still curious. "With Luna at the hospital?"

"Yeah." Tate swallowed another a bite of hot dog. "But I still work out on my own to keep limber. Swim with Mark almost every day. And beat him." He finished his food, then asked, "Who gave you that necklace you always wear?"

Madi's appetite suddenly vanished. She set the rest of her meal aside and stared down at the table. "Karrie. My sister. She died when I was sixteen."

Regardless of how many years had passed, it never got easier to say.

"I'm sorry." Concern flashed in his eyes, stirring feelings she didn't want to revisit. Thankfully he didn't offer the usual platitudes, for which Madi was grateful. But he did take her hand. "How?"

"Overdose."

His long fingers entwined with hers were warm and callused.

He squeezed her hand, and Madi blew out a breath. "You ever lose anyone?"

Tate didn't answer right away. She looked over at him and found him studying a map of Wyckford on the wall. "The last mission I led, there was an explosion. I lost all my team members; plus the people we were sent to rescue." He met her gaze at last. "That was four years ago now. I live with those memories every day."

Throat tight as she struggled to process what that must have been like for him, she said, "I'm sorry."

"The weather conditions were awful that night, and the investigation done after the accident confirmed we had no choice but to go… But still," he continued, "it shouldn't have happened. It was my fault."

Madi frowned. She didn't know a lot about him, but she was sure of one thing. "I'm sure that's not true."

He didn't answer, just stared at the map on the wall. When Tate finally turned to her again, Madi could tell from his closed expression the walls had come down again. He scrubbed a hand over his face. "Look. I'm about as unsafe a choice as you can possibly get for this…" He gestured between them. "Whatever this thing is. You know I'm leaving soon. Wyckford's too quiet."

Yeah. But for some reason, she trusted him. Both the night of the auction and now. She changed subjects to safer topics. "Do you like working on the flight crew?"

"It's what I know." He looked into her eyes, his own unapologetic. "People always need help. When I go back to the Air Force, I'm sure it'll be the same."

When I go back...

Her heart lurched. Which was silly because it wasn't like they were in a long-term relationship or anything. Hell, they'd only had sex once. But the fact he clearly wouldn't be in Wyckford forever was like a bucket of icy water over the head. And a reminder to herself that this was just an interlude.

Her disappointment was undeniable and shockingly painful. Madi had really thought she could do this, keep things casual, but that wasn't the case apparently. She wasn't built for flings. With a sigh, Madi stood. Tate did as well, gathering their garbage and taking it to a trash bin before coming back to stand beside her at the table.

"I can't do this," she whispered.

He nodded. "I know."

"I want to, but I—"

"It's okay." Tate brushed a kiss over Madi's temple. Then he was gone, proving for the second time he was, after all, her perfect Mr. Wrong.

CHAPTER TEN

Two days later, Madi entered the town meeting for the budget presentation in the big central meeting room at Wyckford General. It was full, as they all tended to be.

God forbid anyone in Wyckford miss anything.

Palms sweaty and heart racing, she bit her fingernails through discussions on putting sports and arts back in the schools, getting parking meters along the sidewalks downtown and whether the mayor would run for another term.

Finally, the Health Services Clinic budget was up on the agenda. Bud Lofton stood and reiterated the bare bones of it all and then asked for opinions. Two attendees immediately rushed up in the center aisle to the microphone. The first was Mr. Martin.

"I'm against this idea and always have been." He gripped his cane in one hand and pointed with a bony finger of the other. "It costs us—the hardworking taxpayers—money."

"Actually," Bud interrupted. "The clinic runs mainly off grants, plus donations from the auction and other events throughout the year. Like next week's pumpkin carving contest." He smiled at Madi. "Nurse Scott talked everyone on the board into entering, so I'm expecting you all to come out and support us."

There was a collective gasp of glee.

People *applauded*, and Madi relaxed a bit. Bud's announcement had just guaranteed them a huge showing at the contest. Wyckford was sweet that way.

Still in the aisle, Mr. Martin tapped on the microphone, his face pinched. "I'm still talking! The free clinic brings too many *undesirables* to our town. Addicts. Criminals." His gaze found and zeroed in on Madi in the back. She sank deeper into her seat. "You all need to think about that."

Mr. Martin hobbled back to his chair.

Next up was Sarah Gordon, the town clerk and manager. With what sounded like genuine regret, she said, "I'm also against the clinic, but not for the reasons Mr. Martin stated. I just don't think we need to deplete our limited hospital resources with the Health Services Clinic. While Bud is right about grants and donations making up the bulk of the clinic's budget, it doesn't cover it all. Wyckford General is responsible for the rest of it. And when our library has no funds and our schools are short-staffed due to enforced layoffs, I think we need to take a close, hard look to see if these funds are allocated in the best way possible. I'm sorry, Madi, but it's true."

Some in the audience murmured agreement, and Madi's panic soared.

She couldn't lose the clinic. She'd worked so hard to get it running. It helped so many people who needed it. People like Karrie. There was nothing she could do to save her long-lost sister, but maybe she could prevent someone else from following the same fate...

Then Lucille Munson, in her bright pink tracksuit and brighter white tennis shoes, took the mic. A matching magenta headband held back her steel gray-blue hair. She was so short the microphone stood about a foot above her head. This didn't stop her. She tipped her head up toward the mic, her bun all aquiver. "The HSC serves a very specific and needed function in our community. Because if I thought I had the clap, I have a place to go."

The audience erupted in laughter.

Lucille continued. "And the clinic is in the best hands with Madison Scott. She's a wonderful nurse and has her degree in business as well. She's one smart cookie. I know some of you might think Madison's too sweet to handle such a big responsibility as the HSC." She glared at Sarah Gordon first, then Mr. Martin in the front row. "Or that her programs for drug rehab and teenage pregnancies will cause Wyckford to be overrun by dealers and pimps. But if she can't control the riffraff, then her new boyfriend certainly can."

By this time, Madi had sunk so low in her chair she could hardly see when a tall, broad-shouldered guy in faded jeans took the microphone, which came up to his chest.

Tate.

He spoke in a clear, unrushed tone. "The Health Clinic will improve the quality of life for people who'd otherwise go without assistance."

Another murmur passed through the audience. One naysayer called out, "There's other places for people to get that kind of help."

"Yeah," someone else called out. "People here don't need the HSC."

"Wrong," Tate said bluntly. "On every flight crew and EMT shift, I encounter townsfolk in Wyckford who *do* require exactly the sort of services the HSC provides. Veterans, for instance."

No one said a word now, though it was unclear whether they were scared into silence by Tate's quiet intensity or simply acknowledging the truth of his words.

"There are people right in your own neighborhoods who need help managing their addictions," he went on. "People who don't have a safe place to go away from violence or teens who can't get STD education or birth control. These problems are real and growing, and the Health Services Clinic is an invaluable resource for the entire county." Tate paused and you could've heard a pin drop. "And Lucille's right. You couldn't have a better person running that clinic than Madison Scott. Each of you should be trying to help. I support this budget and I'll even add to it by donating enough money for a program for veterans, where they can get assistance in rehabilitation or job opportunities or simply to reacclimate to society."

Madi gaped.

The place went silent. A real feat when it came to Wyckford. No one even blinked.

As if sensing her scrutiny, Tate turned and met her gaze for one charged beat, then left.

He'd stood up in front of the entire town and defended her. The knowledge washed over her, as she craned her neck to watch him go.

The meeting ended shortly after that, and people rushed Madi with questions. It was another hour before she was free, and as she left, she looked for Tate, but he was long gone.

That night another storm broke wild over Buzzards Bay. He'd had the day off, so Tate had worked on the Chevelle after he'd gotten home. Then he'd decided to take a drive into town to clear his head of a certain warm, sexy nurse.

He'd learned to shelve his emotions when he'd joined the Air Force, long before he'd ever met Madison Scott. But no amount of training could have prepared him for her.

She was a one-woman wrecking crew when it came to the walls around his heart, laying waste to all his defenses. Only a few weeks ago, no one could've convinced him she'd have the power to bring him to his knees with a single look.

And yet she had.

Tate ended up at the café again, thankfully without large trees knocking him in the head. Luna was there also, watching some reality singing competition on the TV mounted high on the café's wall in the far corner. "Come on, judges! Tell it like it is."

She met Tate at a booth with a coffeepot. Normally she looked alert and on guard, but tonight her face was pale and her smile weak. "What can I get you?"

"What kind of pie do you have left?"

She rattled off the selections, then returned two minutes later with a huge slice of apple for him. "Enjoy. Best on the planet, trust me."

Quite the claim, but one bite proved it was true. Tate stopped midway through his second mouthful when he noticed the bloodstained towel wrapped around the palm of Luna's left hand as she refilled his coffee. "Are you okay?"

"Fine."

But her other hand shook, and she looked miserable. "Do you need a doctor?"

"No."

He nodded and continued eating. But when he

was done, he cleared his own plate, bringing it to the kitchen, unable to stop himself from helping. "I'm going to ask you again. Do you need a doctor?"

"It was a silly accident with a knife."

Not an answer. Tate unwrapped her hand and looked down at the cut. "You need stitches. And a trip to the ER."

"No, I don't."

"You have a first aid kit?"

"Yeah."

He nodded. "Get it."

Unfortunately, the Buzzy Bird's supplies consisted of a few Band-Aids and a pair of tweezers, so Tate got his own medic bag from the Chevelle, then returned to the kitchen to tend to Luna's wound. He had Steri-Strips, but the laceration was a little too deep for that.

"Sit down," he told her.

"The café's still open. People might come in."

"They'll wait." She looked a little greener now, so he pushed Luna onto the lone stool in the back. "Put your head down."

She dropped it to the counter instead with an audible *thunk* while Tate disinfected the wound, then opened a tube of skin glue. The stuff stung like hell but would do the job. Luna sucked in a breath as he worked, finally covering her hand with a large waterproof bandage.

"Thanks." Luna let out a shuddery sigh once he was done.

"You're welcome." Tate gestured toward her hand. "How's that feel?"

She opened and closed her fist, testing it. "Better. Thanks." She watched him put everything back into his kit. "You and Madi make a pretty good team."

Before Tate could answer, Mark Bates walked into the kitchen, then stopped, his eyes narrowed on the blood-soaked towel on the counter. "What happened?"

"Nothing." Luna turned her back on him.

Mark looked at Tate then, expecting an answer. "What happened to her?"

"She's declined to say."

"A knife," Luna said over her shoulder. "It was an accident. No big deal. Go away."

There was definite tension in the air between his good friend and Luna. Usually, his friend was affable and easygoing, but now Mark had all sorts of tense body language happening.

Then Luna made an annoyed sound and opened the door, gesturing for them both to leave. For emphasis, she jerked her head, making her wishes perfectly clear.

Mark waited a beat, then walked away, muttering under his breath.

Tate followed, telling himself this was none of his business. She wanted him. He wanted her right back, more than he could have possibly imagined. Right this minute, he could be wrapped up in her sweet, warm limbs, buried deep.

He strode out to the parking lot after Mark, both silent and brooding.

CHAPTER ELEVEN

ON SATURDAY, the free clinic opened as usual. The budget had passed, barely, and Madi knew she had Tate to thank for it. After the town meeting, a handful of locals had pledged more money for certain programs, including one called Drink Responsibly and another for art for seniors. Even one to help counsel the chronically ill. If things kept going the way they were, they might have enough funding to open five days a week to provide crisis counseling. And of course, the Saturday free clinic.

They saw patients nonstop, and later, as Madi closed at the end of the clinic hours, their attending physician for the day, Brock Turner, came out from the back.

After their long day, he looked more rumpled than usual and still had his stethoscope hanging around his neck. His dark hair was tousled too, and his blue eyes lined with exhaustion. But there was also a constant readiness about him that said he wasn't too tired to kick ass if needed. If Madi remembered right, he'd worked a double shift in the ER and a full day of office hours in his own clinic prior to filling in today when their other scheduled volunteer physician had canceled unexpectedly. He'd told Madi before that he did it out of love—both for the job and for taking care of those in need. She was so happy he and Cassie had found each other. They were both wonderful people and made the best parents to Brock's young daughter, Adi.

"Nice job today," he said to Madi.

"Thanks to you."

He shrugged like it was no big deal. He was about the same height as Tate, over six feet and muscled. He might be a workaholic, but he was also the most approachable doctor she'd ever met. And treated the nurses with respect. Such behavior should be automatic, but so often wasn't.

"You're doing something really good here, Madi," Brock said.

She glowed over the compliment later as she locked up. As the last staff member on the premises, she'd walked through each of the rooms, cleaning up a little as she went. They had two of them, plus a small kitchen, and a front reception area large enough for groups to rent when the clinic was closed. They were also in the process of renovating a back storage closet to house the controlled drug lockup, but for now those medications and samples were kept in one exam room in a secure cabinet.

Tomorrow night they'd hold the regularly scheduled AA meeting. Monday night would be Narcotics Anonymous. Wednesday nights hosted a series of guest speakers for teen advocacy programs. All of it made Madi feel useful. Helpful. She hadn't been able to save Karrie, but she could save others.

By the time she locked the front door and got to her car, thunder rolled in the distance. Night had fallen, and the lot wasn't as well-lit as she'd like. She was parked on the back side of the hospital in a narrow side street. She slid behind the wheel just as the rain started and inserted her key in the ignition. Turned it but nothing happened.

Madi tried again and nothing. Dead battery, probably. She peered out and sighed. She was far too tired to walk home in the deluge, plus her feet ached from being on them all day. So, she pulled out her phone and called her brother.

"Yo," Jack Jr. answered. "Bad time."

"I need you to come jump-start my battery. You owe me, Jack. I let you and your idiot friends borrow my car, remember? Maybe this is somehow your fault."

"No, the windshield is my fault. Not the battery."

She noticed a small crack in the glass on the passenger side and felt another eye twitch starting. "Come on. Please. I could really use your help tonight."

"Hang on." Jack Jr. covered the phone and murmured something to someone. A muted female voice laughed, then he was back. "Madi, I'm on a date. With *Allie*."

Then he hung up.

Grinding her teeth, Madi called him back.

He didn't pick up.

"Dammit." She scrolled through her contact list again. Her mother was out of the question. She didn't own a set of jumper cables, let alone know how to use them. Madi dropped everything to help everyone else, and none of them could return the favor. This depressing thought didn't change the fact she was still wet, cold and stranded in a dark parking lot. She thumbed her contacts again, then stopped.

Tate Griffin.

She had his number from the other day when she'd gotten into his records to type up her notes on his suture removal. But she shouldn't call him. For one, they'd had a one-night stand. For two, she liked him. A lot. And for three, she'd started fantasizing about sleeping with him again.

All great reasons not to call him.

But then he *did* know a thing or two about fixing his own vehicle…

With a sigh, she dialed his number, then held her breath. He answered on the fourth ring. "Griffin."

"It's Madi."

He seemed to absorb that information for a moment before she rushed on. "I'm at the clinic and my car won't start. I'm the last one here, and I've tried calling my brother but he's not available and—"

"Lock your doors. I'll be right there."

Madi slipped her phone into her pocket and rested her head on the steering wheel. She was tired. She could really use a foot rub. And a body massage, come to think of it. She'd gotten one at the lovely day spa in town for her birthday last year from Toni. It had been fantastic, but Madi now wondered what it would be like to have Tate work her over instead.

She pictured them on a deserted beach at sunset, Tate in a pair of low-slung board shorts and nothing else, his big hands all over her bikini-clad body, his eyes creased in that way he had of showing his feelings without moving his mouth. Madi smiled up at him as he flipped her over to lie face down on her towel. She felt breathless for him to touch her again. His lips brushed her shoulder, and she wriggled for more. He groaned her name, a whispered warning as he ran a finger down her spine, then between her legs until she writhed with need. She moved with him, seeking more. Then he entered her, and she cried out as he shuddered in pleasure, then collapsed on top of her and—

Rap. Rap. Rap.

Madi jerked upright and banged her head on the sun visor.

Tate waited while she rolled down the window, her face hot.

"Hi," she said. "I was just—"

Dreaming about sex on the beach with you.

"Sleeping?" he asked when she hesitated, one brow quirked.

She nodded and looked away. "Guess I'm tired."

"You look flushed. You're not getting sick, are you?"

She shook her head. "I'm fine."

"Pop the hood for me, and I'll get started." He moved back to the front of the car, seeming not to care that he was getting soaked by the rain.

Madi was glad for a second alone to collect herself. But it didn't take long before Tate was back at her window again.

"Try starting it again," he said. "You'll need a new alternator sooner rather than later."

Whatever that was. "Is it expensive?"

"Not for the part." He wiped his hands on a towel he must've brought from his vehicle. "The labor's what will cost you, but it shouldn't. It's easy enough to replace." He held up a metal stick. "You need oil too." He disappeared back beneath her hood again, asking, "When's the last time you had anyone look at this poor baby?"

"Uh…"

The sounds of him fiddling with her engine were interspersed with mutters of "the lack of respect for the vehicle" and "even if it *is* a piece of crap."

"Who taught you how to do all this car stuff?" she asked, hoping to learn more about him.

"My dad. When he wasn't flying planes for the Air Force. And my mom was a secretary at the Pentagon."

Madi smiled. "A military brat through and through, huh?"

"All I ever knew," he agreed, returning to work on some part under her hood.

"Is that why you wanted to start a program for veterans at the clinic?" she asked. His check had arrived, earmarked for that purpose. Madi had already contacted a good counselor about getting involved, one who could help people like Mr. Ryan. "Where are your parents now?"

"Both gone. My dad died in Desert Storm. My mom a couple of years ago from pneumonia."

"Oh." Her smile faded as he continued to inspect—whatever he was inspecting. "Do you have any siblings?"

"Nope. Just me now." Tate straightened, then closed her hood. "Everything else looks okay, but I'll follow you home just in case."

"There you go again," she said softly, still thinking about him being all alone in the world. "Acting like a hero."

"Make no mistake," he said quietly as he started back to his Chevelle. "I'm nobody's hero."

CHAPTER TWELVE

MADI WATCHED WITH satisfaction as the citizens of Wyckford lined up in the high school gymnasium for the pumpkin carving contest on Sunday. The schedule had been set in advance, and as heavily advertised, every board member had agreed to participate.

They charged a twenty-five-dollar entry fee for everyone and that included your pumpkin, a carving tool, and a T-shirt. Big price tag, but people were paying for the joy of seeing their town hotshots get covered in goo like regular Joe Schmos.

Madi had picked out a medium-sized pumpkin for herself and stood now behind the table near Mark Bates, Brock Turner and Judith. They all were dressed in jeans and Pumpkin Contest T-shirts with a logo designed by Luna as people registered and filled the other tables in the gym.

Mark had brought along his earbuds and was currently bopping to his music as he drew a face on his pumpkin with a black marker.

Luna walked up to Madi, a large pumpkin

tucked under her arm and her carving tool in her hand. "How's it going?"

"Good," Madi said, glancing over at Mark. "Go see what he's drawing."

Instead, Luna cocked her head toward the door. "Maybe you should see what your new boyfriend is up to."

"What?" Madi frowned as she looked over to see Tate walking in, hot as ever with his dark stubble and plenty of attitude.

Tate had been awake since before dawn. He'd gone for a punishing swim with Mark at the beach. Afterward, he'd run, falling only once, and only because a crab had come out of nowhere and startled him. Then, on his way back into town just now, he'd seen a sign for the pumpkin carving contest in support of the clinic and decided to check it out. Seeing Madi in her formfitting orange T-shirt and jeans made it more than worth it. She looked like a girl-next-door-meets-*Maxim* photo shoot.

Drawn like a magnet, Tate got in line and registered. As he collected his T-shirt and carving tool, something loosened deep within him. Tate couldn't have explained the feeling to save his own life.

She'd piled her hair on top of her head for the contest, but it wasn't holding. Loose strands had escaped and curled next to her temples and cheeks and down the back of her neck. He knew how soft her skin was there, and if he put his mouth to the sensitive area, she'd make a little sound that went straight through him. He was crazy in lust with a woman he had no business wanting.

Not that *that* seemed to deter him in the slightest.

"Hey, there!" Madi called as he picked out a pumpkin, then walked toward her table. Before he reached her though, Lucille stopped him.

"My neighbor's got a Charger," the older lady said. "1970, I think. Front-end problems. Told him you might be interested in looking at it. Are you?"

That vintage vehicle was a sweet old thing. Tate wouldn't mind getting his hands on one. "Yep."

"Good." Lucille smiled. "That's right nice of you."

That was him, a right nice guy.

Madi waited until he stopped in front of her, then said, "Thanks for coming."

He smiled, slow and suggestive. Madi went bright red.

"Best get changed," she warned. "You don't want your regular clothes ruined by pumpkin guts."

He laughed and set his pumpkin down, then pulled off his sweatshirt, enjoying her fluster as she tried to look anywhere but at him.

By the time he had the T-shirt on, Madi was busy drawing, so he moved on down the long table until he found an empty spot at the end. Pumpkin carving wasn't something he had much experience with, but he did the best he could and by the time the buzzer went off and he'd gotten elbow deep in gourd guts, he was happy with how his creation had turned out. He'd ended up with a creation that looked like a cross between Freddy Krueger and Kermit the Frog. And if that wasn't terrifying, he didn't know what was.

After grabbing some wet wipes and a towel to clean himself up, he strolled around the tables looking at the other pumpkins, gradually making his way over to where Madi was talking with some of the other townsfolk about the contest. Behind her was a large plastic bucket full of pumpkin guts. Tate walked up and tapped her on the shoulder, and she turned fast. Too fast.

"Oh!" Madi said as she jumped back.

"Watch out." Tate reached for her, but it was too late.

She tripped over the bucket and went down with a little squeal of surprise—straight into the vat of goo.

"Oh, God!" Madi flailed. "Help!"

Brock and Mark, who stood nearby, rushed over, but Tate got to Madi first.

"Are you all right?" he asked, pulling her up.

She stepped back, her hands going to her own butt, now covered in slimy muck. "No worries. I have lots of padding back there."

"You sure?" Brock asked, frowning at her ankle.

"You didn't reinjure the one you broke last year, did you?"

"No." Madi laughed a little, obviously embarrassed. "Just please tell me no one took my picture."

Someone from the other end of the place yelled, "Say cheese…"

Brock swore beneath his breath, making Madi laugh. "Oh, well. What's a little public humiliation for a good cause, eh?"

Then everyone went back to the contest.

Tate waited until they announced the winner—which unsurprisingly wasn't him—and would've said goodbye to Madi, but she was already busy talking to the judges. So, he changed direction and started to walk out, but something made him look at her once more as he left. From across the gym, Madi watched him too, her gaze long and thoughtful.

After the accident, Tate had tried to live with no regrets. But this time, when he left Wyckford, he'd regret leaving Madi Scott behind.

That night, Madi met her friends in their usual booth at the Buzzy Bird, forks in hand.

"So." Cassie licked frosting off her lips. "Arthur Schmidt at the hardware store asked me out the other day."

Madi and Luna busted out laughing.

"Good thing you're engaged to Brock, huh?" Madi winked.

"Yep." Cassie ate another bite of chocolate decadence cake. "How's the drawing coming, Luna?"

Luna shrugged. "Between my schedule at the hospital with PT patients and filling in here when needed, there's not a lot of time for me to do art these days." Then she eyed Madi, changing the subject. "You want to talk about today?"

Madi frowned. "What about it?"

"Gee, I don't know—how you drooled over Tate Griffin at the pumpkin carving contest earlier."

"I did not drool."

"BS," Luna said.

Madi sighed and set down her fork, shrugging. "I like him."

"And that's a bad thing why?" Cassie's brow furrowed. "You're both single, right?"

"Because he's not exactly a forever kind of guy," Madi said. "He's made that clear."

Tate went swimming that night by moonlight. Then he hit the beach for another run. This time he didn't fall. Not once. When he was done torturing his body and his every muscle quivered from exertion, he went home and showered, then went back to bed, hoping he was too tired for nightmares.

Things started out good too. He dreamed about a time his team had been assigned to rescue the passengers of a sinking reconnaissance vessel off the coast of Istanbul. Then the dream shifted to another mission, where they'd used a local fishing boat in Cambodia to reach a stranded airman, which then transitioned a third time to when they'd managed to save a bus, loaded with recent recruits, that had somehow gone off the road and into the Gulf of Mexico.

All successful rescues.

But before long everything went straight to hell once more.

Tate had been thrown from the burning wreckage by the force of the helicopter's explosion. Darkness followed. When he opened his eyes again, his ears rang so loud he couldn't hear anything. A silent horror as wild flames surrounded him.

He swam with all his might, trying to reach what was left of the chopper. On the way, he found Kelly, but she was already dead. Located Tommy and Brad too and did what he could for them, but they passed as well. Then he'd discovered Trevor, their pilot, floating on the other side of the wreckage, gasping for air, his chest crushed and bloody. By the time Tate reached him, all he could do was hold Trevor's hand as his life slowly faded away…

Drenched in sweat, he woke up alone in bed, far from the black churning ocean. He inhaled deep and shoved his fingers through his damp hair. A glance at the device on his nightstand showed it was eight in the morning now. His next shift didn't start until that afternoon, but Tate got up again anyway, tugging on his jeans and shoving his phone and empty Vicodin bottle into his pocket.

It wasn't even dawn yet, but he was too restless to sit still. He grabbed the part from the shelf in his garage, then fired up the Chevelle and drove into town. To Madi's house, a ranch in an older neighborhood with a fresh coat of paint, and her junky car in the drive. Which was why he was here.

Or that's the excuse he was going with anyway.

It took him all of six minutes to replace her alternator with one he'd brought.

Maybe he needed to pick up more shifts with the flight crew or ambulance service to stay busy and feel useful. But there were only so many emergencies in a town the size of Wyckford. He put his tools away and started to get behind the wheel of the Chevelle when he heard the garage door open.

In the lit interior Madi stood with her long brown hair in a wild cloud around her face and shoulders and her bare feet sticking out from beneath the hem of her robe. "Tate? What are you doing here?"

Honestly, her guess was as good as his.

But then, he found himself climbing out of the car and walking up to her.

"Tate?" She frowned up at him, clearly confused. He knew the feeling.

He didn't answer. Waiting to see if she'd tell him he was crazy or gave him the slightest indication he wasn't welcome. If so, he'd leave.

He was good at leaving.

But instead, Madi surprised him by stepping closer, meeting him halfway. Her hand trembled slightly as she reached for him, making him feel very useful indeed.

In the back of his mind, he'd told himself if Madi hadn't started things up between them at the auction, he'd have never slept with her. But deep down he knew that was a lie. It was supposed to have been just one night, but they kept getting in deeper.

She was like a drug. The most addicting kind. He craved her like he'd never experienced before. Tate was pretty sure Madi felt the same about him. He had no idea what to do with that or with his emotions, which got in his way. His whole "no attachment" thing had gone right off the rails, and he felt disconcerted, discombobulated, like his world had turned upside down.

But then his thoughts stopped entirely because her parted lips and flushed cheeks and bedroom eyes told him he affected her every bit as much as she did him. Helpless against the riptide of desire pulling him in, Tate caught Madi to him and stepped over the threshold back into the house, slamming the garage door button and then kicking the door closed behind him.

They staggered into the entryway, mouths fused, bumping into something and knocking it over as she tripped and slammed into the coat rack. They both laughed as Tate spun Madi away from danger, pressing her against a little cherrywood desk. He trapped her there with his body, all amusement fading as she gasped, the sound full of desire.

He wanted to hear it again. Lowering his head, Tate kissed the sweet spot beneath her ear, along her jaw, then the column of her neck. He spent a long moment at the hollow of her throat because, oh yeah, she made the sound once more, her shaky hands clutching his shoulders.

"I dreamed about you," Madi said softly.

Tate was glad, even more so since he had no idea how much he needed this, *her*, until this very minute. "Tell me."

"We were back at the auction." Her fingers glided through his hair, making him shiver. "Working our way through all the furniture."

"Where did we start?" he asked, nibbling her earlobe.

She gasped. "A table."

"Nice." He was hard as a rock. Maybe distance wasn't the way to go. Maybe they could get each other out of their systems. Tate turned her so she faced the small mirror over the desk. Madi watched the reflection as his hands ran down her arms.

The air crackled with electricity. And need. So much need.

"What are you wearing beneath the robe?" he asked.

She bit her lower lip. "Nothing."

Her body was so close to his that a sheet of paper couldn't fit between them. Tate reached her belt. "Do you want this?"

"Yes."

One tug and the robe opened. She didn't take her hungry gaze off their reflection, her eyes glued to Tate's fingers as they bared her body.

"Madi. You're so beautiful." He stroked her stomach, then cupped her breasts, his thumbs brushing her nipples, wringing another gasp out of her. He did it again, his touch light and teasing before he let her go.

She whimpered.

He pushed the robe off her shoulders. Then he pinned her hands in front of her on the desk, which forced her to bend over. He gently squeezed, signaling he wanted her to stay like that.

"Tate—" she choked out, holding the position with a trusting sweetness that nearly undid him, especially combined with the sexy sway of her breasts and the helpless grind of her hips back against him. He cupped those gorgeous full breasts again before skimming one hand south, between her legs, where he found her wet and ready for him.

She gripped the table tight, eyes closed and head back. Then he slid a finger deep inside her, and she gave an inarticulate little cry, straining.

"Tate—" she gasped, breathless. "Please."

Madi trembled as Tate added some pressure with his thumb, kissing along the nape of her neck to her shoulder. She panted, arms taut and face a mask of pleasure.

"Tate."

Madi skittered over the edge, crying out as she shattered, her knees wobbling. Tate caught her, then stripped, putting on a condom before pushing inside her. Her body still quivered from her orgasm, and he bent over her, pressing his torso to her back, brushing his mouth against her neck, giving her a moment. Then she ground against him, restless, and he moved, pushing them both close to the edge again. She met his thrusts, arching her back, demanding more.

His hunger surged, along with a rather shocking, scary, sizzling shot of adrenaline-fueled possessive protectiveness.

You can't protect her.

Still, despite his anxiety, he couldn't stop. Couldn't tear his eyes from their reflection either. He was too far gone. Every nerve ending in his body screamed at him to let go. The fire she'd started inside him flashed bright, a tight ache in his gut. He couldn't hold on much longer. Then Madi went over the edge again and Tate followed, burying his face in her hair as he climaxed so hard his legs buckled.

It was not enough.

It was too much.

It was everything.

He made sure his knees hit the floor and not hers, turning Madi to face him and pulling her in. After a minute, he leaned back to see her face. Her helpless smile tugged one from him as well.

"Good?" Tate asked.

Madi traced a finger along his lower lip. "So much better than good."

CHAPTER THIRTEEN

SHE WASN'T SURE what had brought Tate to her so early in the morning or what he'd been doing out in her driveway, but sitting with him now, naked in her entryway, was a pretty good start to the day.

Madi blushed as he bent in to kiss her. She traced her hand down his torso, over a hip to his upper thigh, and found an unnatural ridge. A jagged scar ran the length of his left leg from groin to knee, and she stilled in horror for what he'd suffered. Their position, with her cuddled up against his chest, couldn't be comfortable for him. "Are you all right?"

"I'm numb from the waist down right now."

She gave a breathless laugh, relieved to feel the usual tension in his big, battle-scarred body lessen. "Good. I know it gives you pain from the accident."

"It wasn't an accident." He paused, then grimaced. "I mean it was, but it was preventable."

She frowned. "Preventable how?"

"If I'd chosen not to go out there in the first place, my team would be alive today."

Her throat tightened at the guilt and remorse edging his tone now. "But didn't you say those airmen would've died if you hadn't gone?"

"Yes, but they died that night anyway. I could have at least saved my team."

Madi took that in a moment, letting the silence settle around them for a while. Finally, she said, "That must have been awful for you. Alone out there, injured."

"It was. I had cracked ribs, a broken wrist, and a collarbone fracture. Some internal injuries and the leg. All survivable." He paused again. "Unlike everyone else."

Survivor's guilt. I know it well.

Aching for the physical and emotional pain he'd endured, Madi ran her fingers lightly over his chest, feeling the fine tremor of his muscles. Aftershocks of great sex or bad memories, it was hard to tell.

"It wasn't your fault, Tate," she said softly. "You were forced to make an impossible decision."

"Madi." He shook his head. "I *really* don't want to talk about this."

"I know." She clutched the infinity charm around her neck. "I don't like to talk about what happened to my sister Karrie either. For a long time after she was gone—after I failed to save her—I couldn't bear to remember her, much less talk about her."

He gave a long, shuddery exhale, then drew her in closer, burying his face in her hair. "You said she overdosed?"

"Yeah. She was eighteen," she said, closing her eyes against the sting of tears. "And pregnant."

"Oh, Madi." He tightened his grip on her. "Please don't tell me you think what she did was your fault."

"We were sisters. I knew she was having problems. I should have—"

"No." He pulled back to look into her eyes. "There's nothing you could have done. *Nothing.* You were just a kid yourself."

She could barely speak. "How do you get past it?"

"I'm still figuring it out. But you keep going. You keep moving. You keep living."

Tate woke up a little while later, on his back, the wood floor stuck to his spine and a warm, sated woman curled into his side. Somehow, he staggered to his feet, then scooped up Madi. The first rays of sunlight were just visible over the horizon.

"No," she murmured, her words slurring from exhaustion as she stirred in his arms. "Not time to get up yet."

He'd seen the rosters in the ER the other day and knew she'd been working around the clock, twelve hours and more at a time. "Shh," he whispered against her temple. "Sleep."

"Tate?" Groggily, she slipped her arms around his neck. "Where are we going?"

"Bed." He planned to tuck her in, then get the hell out of there before he did something stupid like fall asleep with her. Sex was one thing. Sleeping together afterwards turned it into something else entirely.

You idiot, it's already something else...

On her bed were the two big stuffed animals he'd won for her at the arcade. An odd feeling went through him, warm and cozy, followed closely by wry amusement. He put her down and started to straighten, but she tugged him down with her.

"Cold." She shivered and tried to burrow against his body.

Giving in, Tate pulled her close for a minute, yanking the comforter over them. He'd share his body heat until she fell back to sleep, then he'd head out.

Madi pressed her face into his throat, tucking her cold toes behind his calf. "Feels good."

"I'm not staying," he warned, not knowing which one of them he was telling.

Two minutes later, her breathing slowed into the deep slumber of the exhausted.

She was out for the count.

And all over him.

Her hair was in his face, her warm breath puffing gently near his jaw, her bare breasts flattened against his side and chest. She had one hand tucked between them, the other low on his stomach. Plastered to him like a second skin.

Lulled in by her soft, giving warmth, he closed his eyes and fell asleep.

At some point, the nightmare gathered, pulling him in. Luckily, he woke up before he made a complete ass of himself. It was still early by the sunshine slanting in through the blinds. Rolling off the bed, Tate walked out into the entryway to grab his jeans when he felt the hand on his arm. He jumped and whipped around to face Madi. Unable to help himself, he twitched free, and the front doorknob jabbed him hard in the back. "Ouch."

"Sorry. Didn't mean to startle you." Silhouetted by the rising sun behind her, Madi stayed a short distance away, concern pouring off her in the same way passion had earlier. "Okay?"

He could've lied. Added a small smile and a kiss, to make sure she bought it.

But he didn't want to get close. He shoved his feet into his shoes and grabbed his wallet and keys as he saw Madi put on his shirt.

"Tate?"

He opened the front door and headed outside. She padded after him onto the porch, her fingers running down his bare back.

"Did you have a bad dream?"

He stilled. "No." *Yes.*

"The night in the storm," she said quietly. "You had a nightmare. Did it happen again here?"

"No." He dropped his head to the door. "That's not it."

"Then what's wrong?"

He straightened. "I have to go, Madi."

"Stay. Sleep with me. I won't tell."

Tate knew she only wanted to help. But he didn't want it. He was fine. All he needed was to be left alone. That was for the best. "Can't."

"But—"

He pulled open the door and stepped into the chilly morning, leaving before he couldn't anymore.

Madi plopped back onto her bed and stared up at the ceiling, haunted by Tate's expression when he'd left. This whole thing with him was supposed to have been fun. A little walk on the wild side. But it had become so much more. She was good at healing people.

But with Tate… She couldn't heal him, any more than she'd been able to heal herself.

Madi showered and changed, then went to work. A few hours in, she was paged to the nurses' station.

"What's up?" she asked Camilla, who sat behind the desk when she got there.

Camilla hiked her chin toward the hallway. Madi found a familiar man propped against the wall, his stance casual, his body relaxed. But she knew better.

"I'm on break," she said, then walked toward Tate. "Hey."

"Hey." His eyes never wavered from hers. "Got a minute?"

"Sure." All too aware of Camilla's eyes—and ears—on them, Madi gestured for him to follow her to the staff room where they sat in the corner. It was too early for the lunch crowd, so they had the place to themselves, except for a janitor working his way across the floor with a mop.

Tate's knee brushed against hers beneath the table. He was dressed in his flight crew uniform now, probably on his way to work.

He looked edible.

And she was afraid he was here to tell her he was leaving.

"You want anything?" she asked, pointing to the vending machines. "Coffee? Tea?" *Me*...

"No, thanks. Listen, Madi." He stared at her, his green-gold gaze fathomless, giving nothing away. "I wanted to apologize for earlier." He caught her hand. "I acted like an idiot."

She sank back into her seat. "I understand, you know."

"I'm sorry about Karrie," he said. "But you deserve better from me."

Before she could respond, the elevator music on the overhead PA system was replaced by an authoritative male voice. "Code Red."

They both jumped up. Code Red meant there was a fire, and personnel were to report in immediately. Today was a scheduled drill but Madi hadn't expected it now. Great timing.

"Code Red," the voice repeated. "All personnel respond immediately. Code Red. *Repeat, Code Red.*"

CHAPTER FOURTEEN

WITH THE HOSPITAL in temporary lockdown because of the fire drill, Tate went to his appointed station and waited. Soon, firefighters and other emergency personnel came pouring in. Ten minutes later, the hospital employees reappeared, without Madi.

Two women in scrubs stood near him, looking at him, then whispering to themselves, clearly gossiping, probably about him and Madi. Perfect. He'd tried to make her life easier while he was here, and all he'd done was make things worse.

He shouldn't have messed around with her life. He'd be gone soon, but Wyckford was Madi's home, her world. Tate felt confused and uncertain, two foreign emotions for him. He'd started to believe *he* was the one giving here, the experienced one imparting a little wildness and the dubious honor of his worldly ways. How magnanimous.

Especially since the truth was Madi had done all the giving, schooling him in warmth, compassion and strength. In the process, she'd wrapped him around her little finger with her soft voice and a backbone of steel.

Dammit. He headed out, slowing at the front entrance. A donation box had been placed there for the Health Services Clinic. He'd given money for the veterans program already, but he knew now exactly what he'd do to give back to the woman who'd given him so much.

The next day Tate brought the sick vet, Mr. Ryan, dinner. He'd found the man out on the street, having left his daughter's somewhere in the night, and—per Mr. Ryan's wishes—moved him into a halfway house outside of town instead. Mr. Ryan had said he didn't want to be a burden on his family anymore, so Madi had arranged a room for him at the halfway house through HSC. It was infinitely better, and safer, than being homeless.

After they ate, Mr. Ryan asked Tate for a ride to the free clinic.

"What's going on here?" Tate asked as they pulled up to the hospital.

"A meeting."

The sign on the front door of the west wing read Narcotics Anonymous.

As he walked the old vet up to the door, Tate noticed someone had attached a sticky note to the sign that said EMPHASIS ON THE "A", PEOPLE!

Tate didn't know whether to be amused that

only in Wyckford would the extra note be necessary or appalled that the town could not keep anything *anonymous* at all.

But part of any twelve-step process was learning to trust, so…

He turned to Mr. Ryan, who'd gone still beside him, seemingly frozen in place.

"I'm too old for this," the vet muttered.

"How old *are* you?" Tate asked.

"Two hundred and fifty."

Tate snorted. "Then you're in luck. They don't cut you off until you're three hundred."

A ghost of a smile touched Mr. Ryan's mouth. "I'm fifty-eight."

Twenty years older than Tate. The vet's body trembled from detoxing. Not good. Tate would've paid big bucks to be anywhere else right now but figured if Mr. Ryan was using him as a crutch, he had to be in a bad way. "How long since your last hit?"

"I ran out of OxyContin four days ago. Doctor says I don't need it anymore."

Without thinking, Tate slipped his hand into his pocket and touched the ever-present empty bottle of Vicodin there. Three years, two weeks, and counting. He thought about saying he'd wait outside, but that felt cowardly, so he went in.

They both survived the meeting. An hour later they exited in silence. Tate didn't know about Mr. Ryan, but he was more than a little shaken by the stories he'd heard, the utter destruction of the lives those people in there had been trying to reboot and repair. He felt grateful he hadn't been one of them. Not completely anyway.

He was almost back to the halfway house when the old vet finally spoke again. "Are you and that cute ER nurse a thing?"

"Madi, you mean?" Tate had been asked this so many times since the auction. By the clerk at the grocery store. By the people he helped on his EMT runs. By basically everyone who'd crossed his path. The very same people who—until he'd met Madi—had been content to just stare at him.

She was the heart and soul of this town, or at least what it would look like in human form. And maybe Tate had thought she'd be someone he could easily walk away from. But he knew now, deep down, that wasn't the case. *She* was different. The big problem was, Madi was grounded here in Wyckford, while *he* would need to decide about leaving soon. The one-night stand had been Madi's idea. Though she'd also accepted his latest visit as an addendum to the original deal. And she'd let him off the hook for being an idiot.

"No," he finally said to Mr. Ryan, hoping to squash any further interest the man might have. "We're not a thing."

"Huh." The vet scratched his scruffy jaw. "Does she know that?"

"Yeah. She knows."

But do you?

"She's a real nice lady," Mr. Ryan continued. "When I was living on a bench at the park, she brought me food at night. Did she ever tell you that?"

Tate shook his head, his chest a little tight at the thought of Madi, after a long day in the ER, seeking out Mr. Ryan to make sure he was fed.

"She can't cook," Mr. Ryan told him with a small smile. "But I ate whatever she brought anyway. Didn't want to hurt her feelings."

Tate shook his head, grinning to himself.

"If I was younger and—" Mr. Ryan shrugged "—*different*, I'd try for her. She's something special. Way too special for the likes of me, though, you know?"

Yeah. Tate knew. He knew *exactly*.

"One time she came to the park and some kids were throwing rocks at me. Madi chased them away. I still think I looked better than she did. Her hair was all over the place, and she was in her scrubs. She looked like a patient from the place I'd stayed in after I got back from my third tour."

A mental facility. Tate pictured Madi furious and chasing off a bunch of bullies.

"You've seen the stuff on Facebook, right?" Mr. Ryan asked.

Tate slid him a side glance. "How are you getting on Facebook?"

"There's a community computer at the halfway house." The old vet smiled. "The town has a homepage. There's a pic up of you two. You two seem awful cozy for not being a thing."

Yeah. Except what he'd had with Madi was the opposite of cozy.

It was hot. Bewildering.

Staggering.

He dropped Mr. Ryan off at the halfway house, then went back to his rental place. He showered and changed, then saw a missed call on his phone and got a little rush at the thought maybe Madi had called him, or they needed him for an extra shift with the ambulance service.

But the message wasn't from either of them. It was from Brock, reminding him he was due in for a recheck of the scar tissue in his leg, per his VA medical records.

The next morning, Tate got his scans, then went to Brock's GP office on the same grounds as the hospital. He checked in at the front desk and was told to wait. He'd perfected the art of hurry up and wait in the Air Force, so when he was finally led back to the office and then the man himself strode in carrying a thick file containing Tate's medical history, he didn't react.

Brock was in full doctor mode today. Dark blue scrubs, a white coat, a stethoscope around his neck, and his ID clipped to his hip pocket. Hair rumpled, eyes tired, he dropped Tate's chart on his desk and sprawled out into his chair. "God, I'm exhausted."

"Long day already?"

"Is it still morning? I don't know anymore." Brock scrubbed his hands over his face. "Adi has started asking questions about where babies come from, and if you know anything about my daughter, she's persistent as hell."

"Oh." Tate grinned. "So, what's the verdict on my scar tissue?"

"Scans show improvement. I think all the exercise you're getting with Mark helps. Keep it up."

Another month in Wyckford might kill him. "I have to let the Air Force know if I'm re-upping for another stint soon."

Brock gave him a look. "You're not planning on leaving, are you?"

"I was *always* planning on going eventually."

"But *now*?"

Tate sighed as Madi's face flashed in his mind. Her looking up at him while lying snuggled against him in her bed, wearing only a soft, sated smile and a slant of moonlight across her face.

"Does Madi know about your plans?" Brock asked quietly.

"This has nothing to do with her," Tate lied.

Brock shook his head, looking baffled. "And reenlisting is what you want to do?"

Tate didn't know. He didn't know much of anything anymore. This thing with Madi had rattled him to his core.

"You know," Brock said in his infuriatingly calm, professional voice. "I'm on the hospital board and there's talk of making your flight para-medic position permanent and giving it a title. Team Leader. The board wants to expand the ser-vice to more rural areas and even transfer cases between Wyckford General and Boston. I could put your name in if—"

"I'm not interested."

Brock stared at him.

Tate held the other man's gaze steadily.

With a shake of his head, Brock stood. "Then I guess we're done here for now."

Tate spent two days *not* making any plans for his future. First, he needed to finish up the Charger for Lucille's neighbor. Then he made some easy repairs around the rental home. After that, there were no excuses left and Tate decided to give him-self a day off from thinking at all.

Which turned into yet another day…

Then he woke up to a message from Brock to stop by his office at ten that morning. Tate swam. Then he ran, hard. Then he worked out with Mark at the gym for an hour until they were both sweat-ing and exhausted. Finally, Tate took a shower and drove to Brock's office.

When he was led back to the office, Brock

looked up from the mountain of paperwork on his desk and scowled at Tate. "You give word to the Air Force yet?"

"No."

Brock gave him a long look, steepling his fingers as he studied Tate like a specimen on a slide. "Why not?"

"Haven't had time." Tate straightened his leg, then winced.

"Hmm." Brock's tone was dry. "I was at the gym this morning too, but you never even noticed me. You were too busy wiping the floor with Mark. You overdo it there?"

"I pulled something."

Brock shook his head. A silent beat passed, then two. Finally, he said, "Maybe I spoke too soon about your scar tissue. I think I should check you one more time in a week before I clear you to return to duty."

Tate agreed, then left by the back exit, which meant he stood in the bright late autumn sunshine in the hospital parking lot staring at Madi's car. He wondered what was wrong with him, but since that was too big of a problem to solve in this decade, he went home. He hadn't been called in for any extra shifts in a while now because things were slow. So, he went out to the garage and fiddled with the Chevelle until it was dark. He'd just gotten back inside when someone knocked on his door.

Madi.

She gave him a small, sweet smile. "Hey."

Chronic idiot. That's me.

"Hey yourself."

She stepped over the threshold and bumped into him since he hadn't moved. He thought it was an accident, but then her hands brushed over his chest and abs. No accident there.

Nor was the fact that she wore that fuzzy pink sweater again, with low-riding jeans and a pair of high heels that brought her up enough to perfectly align their bodies. Her pulse beat like a drum at the little dip in the base of her throat. Tate ran a finger over that spot now, feeling her heart race even faster.

"I talked to Mr. Ryan this afternoon."

Tate lifted his gaze.

"He was back in the ER," she said.

Concerned, Tate frowned. "What happened? Is he all right?"

"Someone caught him wandering around on the highway last night and brought him in. He had a bottle of whiskey and some dope he'd scored somewhere." She put her hand on Tate's, squeezing reassuringly. "He's fine. He's sleeping it off, but before that…he was talking. He said you took him to the NA meeting. And you stayed."

Tate could've lied and said the old vet needed assistance, but he didn't. He waited for Madi's expression to change but she only nodded. No leaping to conclusions, no trial and jury, no pity, nothing.

"Why don't you just ask me what you really want to know, Madi."

"Okay." She drew a deep breath. "Are you an addict, too?"

Tate slipped his hand into his pocket to touch the ever-present Vicodin bottle. It was empty and weighed nothing. Both those things reassured him. He'd messed up plenty, but not that way. "I had a lot of pain and they put me on heavy narcotics after the accident four years ago. I was a wreck."

"You'd just lost your team," she said softly.

Something warm inside him unfurled. Madi was defending him. To *himself*. "I knew if I wanted to have any kind of life again, I had to get off the pain meds, especially to work as a paramedic." He paused, remembering. "It was hard though. I liked the oblivion. Too much."

Her eyes stayed steady on his as she absorbed his words, seeming to take them in without judgment. "That's why you refused narcotics the night of the storm."

Tate nodded. "I stopped taking Vicodin three years ago because I found myself living for the clock again, just waiting for the minute I could take another pill. That's when I quit."

"You went cold turkey?"

"I did." He flashed a grim smile and blew out a breath. "And I still crave it sometimes."

She went quiet for a moment, then said, "The craving part is normal. I gave up chocolate once and the cravings *sucked*."

He choked out a laugh. "I don't think it's exactly the same, Madi."

They both smiled now.

Madi sighed. "I think it helps to keep busy. I know that much."

"I've been distracted plenty lately." Tate rocked back on his heels and her cheeks flamed.

"You must be Wyckford's new go-to mechanic. Lucille said you're helping a friend of hers with his Charger," she commented, glancing at a grease stain on his T-shirt. "Were you working on your own car just now?"

"Yep. Want to see?"

She nodded, and he took her hand and guided her out to the garage.

"What were you doing?" Madi asked as she looked around at the Chevelle and the slew of tools scattered across his worktable.

"Brake lines."

"Show me," she said.

"You want to learn how to put in new stainless steel brake lines?" he asked, heavy on the disbelief as he looked pointedly at her high heels again. "Madi, those shoes aren't meant for working on a car."

"What are they meant for?"

"Messing with a man's head."

Then he figured, what the hell. She saw blood and guts every single day. A little dirt wasn't going to bother her. He grabbed a forgotten sweatshirt off the bench and handed it to her. "Put this on to keep from getting dirty."

She did and it fell to her thighs. "It smells like you."

The odd pressure in his chest increased to a yearning ache that had everything to do with the woman standing in front of him. "And now it's going to smell like *you*."

He kicked over the mechanic creeper, then his backup creeper, and gestured for her to lie down on one of them. When they were both flat on their backs, she grinned over at him. "Now what?"

"Under the car."

She slid herself beneath the Chevelle, and he joined her. Side by side, they stared up at the bottom of the chassis. Then he looked over at her sweet profile and reminded himself he was leaving Wyckford soon. Tate handed her a roll of brake line. "Bend it to fit the contours of the frame as you go." He pointed out the route, and Madi began to work.

"It's peaceful under here," she said. Tate slid her a dubious look, and she laughed. "I'm serious. You don't think so?"

It was grimy, stuffy…and yeah. Peaceful. "I do. I'm just surprised you think so too."

"You don't think I enjoy getting dirty once in a

while?" She bit her lower lip as her cheeks flushed pink, and she laughed at his raised brow. "You know what I mean."

When she had trouble bending the line, he put his hands over hers to help. "Unravel another foot or so."

They worked in companionable silence until she asked, "What was the first car you fixed?"

Tate smiled at the memory. "When I was fourteen my dad bought a Pontiac GTO. Man, she was sweet."

"She?" Madi turned her face to him, and he stroked a rogue strand of hair from her temple, tucking it behind her ear.

"Cars are always female. Do you want to hear this story or not?"

"Yes." She nudged his shoulder with hers. "Go on."

"I took apart the engine."

"Oh, my God." Her brown eyes widened. "Was he mad?"

"It was a classic and in mint condition. *Mad* doesn't even begin to cover my dad's reaction."

Madi blinked at him. "Why'd you do it then?"

Tate still remembered the look on his father's face—the complete shock at the empty engine compartment, the horror that his baby had been breached and violated and then the sheer fury. "I liked taking things apart and putting them back together again. I hadn't meant to take it so far, but I kept undoing and undoing…"

"What happened?"

"I thought my dad would kill me." Tate smiled. "But we ended up rebuilding it together."

She touched his jaw, cupping it in her palm and lightly running the pad of her thumb over the stubble on his chin. "I like being under a car with you."

Working on cars was familiar ground. His constant. But Madi had squeezed herself right into his safety zone, then into his heart. Because no matter what he told himself, he liked being here with her, too.

"What are you scared of?" she asked.

You, he nearly said. And it was true.

Instead, he let out a short laugh. "In general?"

Her eyes softened, and she slid her hand around his nape, bringing him a full-body shiver of pure pleasure. "Yes."

"Being trapped." He rolled out from beneath the Chevelle, then crouched beside Madi's creeper and yanked her out by the ankles.

She sat up and pushed her hair back to meet his gaze. "I know this isn't your home, Tate. That you're going back to the Air Force soon—"

"Madi—" He put his finger over her lips.

She pulled his hand away, keeping a hold on his wrist. "No, it's okay. You're not the small-town type."

And yet here he was, still here in Wyckford.

CHAPTER FIFTEEN

THE NEXT MORNING, Madi woke to Violet's disgruntled *meow*, letting the world know it was past time for her breakfast. When she ignored this, the cat batted her on the forehead with a paw. "Shh."

Meow.

Madi stretched, her body sore from being with Tate the night before. She sighed blissfully and rolled over. She hadn't gotten home until late. Or early, depending on how you looked at it. She'd have liked to stay at his place all night, but that would have been too much.

Not for her. For *him*.

She'd promised him this was a simple fling. No use telling him she'd broken that promise. Besides, she loved being with him. That was the bottom line. The only line. There were no preconceived notions on how they should behave. It was freeing, exhilarating.

Amazing.

Also unsettling. Madi was playing in the big girls' sandbox now with Tate, and she was going to get hurt. Nothing to be done about that though, so she got up and got ready for her workday. When she went to the closet for her white nurses' shoes, she pulled them out, then sniffed, wrinkling her nose, then scowling at the cat. "Oh, no, you didn't."

Violet sat in the middle of the bed, daintily washing her face. She had no comment.

"You *pooped* in my shoe?"

Violet gave her a don't-come-home-late-again look, then continued grooming herself, completely unconcerned about ramifications because they both knew there wouldn't be any.

Madi cleaned up the mess, then grabbed her phone off the nightstand and headed out to her car.

Her brother stood in her driveway with her car hood open, frowning. "Who did your alternator?"

"No one." Madi frowned. "What are you doing? You said you were busy."

"And now I'm not. I picked up a used one for you this morning, but someone beat me to it."

"What?" She peeked at the thing he pointed at, the one shiny, clean part of the whole engine.

"Brand new too," Jack Jr. said.

Her mind flashed back to finding Tate in her driveway in the middle of the night. She'd never questioned his reasons for being there, figuring it had been about sex. But she got a little warm fuzzy now knowing it hadn't been *all* about sex.

Madi drove to work smiling. She parked and went into the ER.

Five minutes into her shift, Judith called her

into her office and laid a piece of paper on her desk, a receipt for ten grand. "Anonymous donation for HSC."

"Wow." Madi sank into a spare chair. "Am I looking at all those zeros correctly?"

"Yes. Well done."

Madi glanced at her boss again, astonished. "How do you know I had anything to do with this?"

Judith smiled. "Because without you there would be no free clinic."

The words rang through Madi's head for the next few hours as she dealt with her patients. Tate was working today too. She saw him several times with the regular ambulance crew when they brought in a new case. First up was a bad case of food poisoning. Then a teenager who'd let her new tattoo get infected. And a woman who was eight months pregnant and ate a jar of pickles, putting herself into labor with gas pains.

They didn't have time to talk though, since Madi was pretty much run ragged for the rest of the day until there was finally a lull in the afternoon. She used the rare quiet time to sit at the nurses' station and catch up on charting.

"Madi!"

She looked up to find one of her regular patients, Jodi Larson, beaming from ear to ear. Jodi was ten, a leukemia patient, and one of Madi's all-time favorite people. She'd been upstairs to the oncology department for her six-month check and based on the smile also on Jodi's mom's face, the news had been good.

"Officially in remission," Jodi said proudly.

Her mom's eyes shone bright as she nodded affirmation of the good news. Thrilled, Madi hugged them both tight, and Jodi presented her with a plate of cookies. "Chocolate chip and walnut. I baked them just for you."

They hugged again. Before Madi could say much else, she got paged—by her own mother.

"Madison." Her mother dragged Madi into a far, quiet corner of the staff break room. "Are you still seeing that man?"

Lucille walked by in her volunteer uniform. "I hope so. Tate Griffin's the hottest thing you've dated since…well, ever. And it's about time Madi stops being the one everyone depends on and finds someone to depend on herself."

Her mother stared at Madi for a long beat, looking stricken. "Is that what this is about?"

Before Madi could answer, Lucille said, "Your next patient's ready for you."

Mr. Martin. Again.

"You," he said when Madi entered his room.

"Me," she agreed and reached for the blood pressure cuff. "Your chart says you passed out after your bath today. Did you take your meds at the right time?"

"I did. I'm not a complete idiot. They didn't work."

"Did you space them out with food, as explicitly instructed on the bottles?"

Mr. Martin glared at her.

"I'll take that as a no." The man's color was off, and his blood pressure was far too low. Both red flags for Madi. "When was your last meal?"

"Hmph."

"Mr. Martin." She put her fingers on the man's narrow, frail wrist to check his pulse. "Did you eat lunch today?"

He straightened in his bed, quivering with indignity. "I know what I'm supposed to be doing."

Madi glanced into his rheumy, angry eyes and her heart clenched. Her instincts said the real problem was the older man didn't have any food, and he probably wasn't feeling good enough to take care of himself, since he'd long ago scared off family and friends with his mean, petty, vicious ways. Madi picked up the phone attached to his bed rail and called the cafeteria. "I need a full dinner tray for trauma room three in the ER."

When the food came, Madi stood beside her grumpy patient. "Eat."

Mr. Martin tried to push it away, but Madi held it still this time. The man's eyes burned bright with temper, which she was happy to see because it meant he already felt better. She leaned closer. "I'm stronger, and *I've* eaten today."

"Well, *that's* obvious." Mr. Martin sniffed at the juice on the tray. "Hmph."

"It's apple."

"I have eyes in my head, don't I?" He sipped and within sixty seconds, his color improved. "You didn't used to be so mean. I'm ready to leave now."

"You can't go home until you eat."

"You're making that up. This cafeteria food isn't fit for a dog," Mr. Martin complained.

"Fine." Madi went to the staff kitchen, pulled out her own lunch and brought it back to the room. "Try my sandwich. Turkey and cheese with spinach. There's a little bit of mustard and probably too much mayo on it, but cholesterol is the least of your problems." Madi also tossed down a baggie of baby carrots and apple slices.

Mr. Martin took a bite of the sandwich first. "Awful," he said, but took another bite. Then another, until there was nothing left but a few crumbs.

"The carrot sticks too," Madi said.

"Are they as horrid as the sandwich?"

"They're as horrid as your bad attitude. And you will eat it all, even if I have to make you."

"Nurse Scott!" a shocked voice said from the doorway.

Judith. *Perfect.*

Madi turned, but not before she saw the evil glee in Mr. Martin's eyes. She jabbed a finger toward the carrots. Mr. Martin meekly picked one up.

In the hall, her boss led Madi out of hearing range of the patient. "What are you doing?"

"Trying a new tactic," Madi said, channeling her inner Tate. He was always so confident and assertive. It made her want to emulate that herself. "Did he finish it all?"

Judith went back to peer around the door, then returned, shaking her head and grinning. "Every bite."

By the time Madi left work that day, she was starving and dead tired. She solved the first problem by eating a handful of Jodi's cookies. Then she eyed the remaining ones before driving to Tate's.

His garage door was open, and the man himself was flat on his back beneath his car, one long denim-clad leg straight out, the other bent. His black T-shirt had risen or maybe his Levi's had sunk indecently low. Either way, the revealed strip of washboard abs and vee of muscle at his hips made her mouth water. She thought about standing there and watching him all night, but after the day she'd had, Madi couldn't imagine he'd enjoy looking at her in return.

Not that Tate had ever said she looked anything other than beautiful. She was stymied. His attraction to her was apparently based on some intangible thing she couldn't fathom. She couldn't get used to the fact that no matter what she did or what she looked like, he seemed to want her. And the feeling was far too mutual.

CHAPTER SIXTEEN

TATE SAT UP on the mechanic's creeper and took in the sight of Madi standing there with a plate of cookies he hoped were for him.

All he could think about was her face down on his bed, boneless and sated with bliss. He'd stroked the damp hair from her face, and she'd smiled in her sleep. His heart had constricted at her arrival, and he'd thought, *Christ, I am in trouble*.

He'd been torn by the urge to tug her close and the urge to retreat. In the end, it hadn't been his choice at all because she'd awakened and gotten dressed to go. He'd followed her home to make sure she got there safely, then driven back to his place and missed her.

Clearly, he was losing it.

He had no idea what she was thinking now, but he hadn't expected her to smile at the sight of him, a smile filled with...

Relief, he realized, and surprise that he was still here.

Yeah, join the club. He was surprised, too.

She still had on her purple scrubs and white Nikes from the ER. She had two pens sticking out of her hip pocket, one red, one black, with corresponding ink marks on the material. She followed his gaze and sighed. "I'm a mess. Don't ask."

"Not a mess," he said. "Are those cookies?"

"Yes. And I had to fight off the staff to keep them for you." She crouched at his side, holding the plate out for him. He took a big bite of one and moaned in deep appreciation.

"Did you give the HSC ten thousand dollars?" she asked.

He'd hoped she wouldn't find out, but that was unrealistic in a town like Wyckford. Taking his time, Tate ate cookie number two, then reached for a third, but she snatched the treats away.

"Did you?"

He eyed her for a long moment. "Which answer will get me the rest of the cookies?"

Madi looked worried as she lowered the plate for him again. "You already gave a donation."

"Your clinic needs it, right?" he asked around another bite.

"But it's *so* much money."

"Don't worry. I can afford it." She just stared at him, so he shrugged and continued. "I can. I get good pay from the Air Force, plus disability from the accident. I'm thrifty and I save."

Madi huffed, then kissed his cheek, but he turned his head and caught her mouth with his.

They were both gratifyingly out of breath by the time they pulled apart.

"Thank you," Madi whispered.

"You're welcome," Tate said, as she rose and went to sit on the stool at his workbench.

"Don't let me keep you from what you were doing. I'll watch."

He arched a brow at her, surprised. "You want me to get back under the car?"

"Absolutely."

Humoring them both, he lay back down onto the mechanic's creeper and rolled back beneath the chassis. Tate heard Madi get to her feet and walk closer, peering into the opened hood above him as she said, "There was another board meeting today at the hospital. They approved making your position permanent on the paramedic flight crew."

She was as see-through as glass. Which in hindsight made her a hell of lot more dangerous than he'd thought. "Yeah? Good for them."

She squatted at his side. "Sounds like the perfect job for you."

Her hand settled on his bad thigh. It'd been only recently that he'd even gotten more sensation back in it, but he was having no trouble feeling anything now. An odd mix of anxiety and anticipation flooded his system. He didn't like where this was going.

"I know Brock gave them your name to consider," she said. "I told Bud you have my vote too."

That had him setting down his wrench and pulling himself back out from beneath the car. Madi was still crouched low as he frowned up into her face. "Why?"

"Because you're probably the most qualified person I know. And if you wanted choices then—"

"I don't want choices. I'm going back to the Air Force."

Madi went still, staring at him with those eyes he'd never been able to resist. "You don't have to."

He met her expressive gaze and felt a stab of pain right in the gut. He'd survived pararescue training. He'd lived through a plane crash. He'd kept on breathing when the rest of his team and the victims they'd been sent to save hadn't done the same. But he didn't know how to do this. "I can't do this, Madi. I'm sorry."

"Why?" she asked in disbelief. "Because you've never explained it to me."

Well, hell.

Chalk it up to the panic now fizzing through his veins like sparklers. Whatever he did here, whatever he came up with, he needed her to want to keep her distance. Except Madison Scott was incapable of distance when her heart was involved. That was both painfully attractive and terrifying. "Madi, I was up-front with you from the start about me and about all this being temporary. I'm not a good fit for you or for that job. Trust me."

She sucked in a breath like he'd slapped her. "So, what? You'll just keep running back to the Air Force for the rest of your life?"

"Maybe."

Madi stared at him, then turned away again.

Tate rose to his feet and walked around to see her face. "C'mon. Let's finish this."

With a sigh, Madi shook her head and put a finger to her twitching eye. "Dammit," she muttered, then looked up at him. "Don't you get lonely, being on your own all the time?"

"But I'm not alone. Not with you around, anyway," he said, and made her laugh.

"Stop it," she said. "This isn't funny."

He drew her closer. "Done being mad at me?"

"Yes."

"Good." Tate knew he had no right to touch her, crave her like air, but he did. And when he kissed her, tasted her, he knew she'd been made for him. Which meant he was far more screwed than he'd even imagined.

But suddenly Madi pulled free, shaking her head. "Tate—stop. I can't. I can't do this and keep it…not real."

"It's real."

"Yes, but real for you means sex with no strings. Real for me means…" She rubbed her chest as if it hurt, then closed her eyes. "Never mind." She took a step back and then another. "I'm sorry, this is my fault. I shouldn't have—"

"Madi—"

"No, it's okay. I'm going now."

Tate watched her get into her car and drive off and knew it was time to make that call to the Air Force. Past time.

CHAPTER SEVENTEEN

AFTER A SLEEPLESS NIGHT, Madi worked a long shift, then took a detour home by Mr. Martin's house. Last night the HSC had hosted a healthy living seminar given by a local dietician, and he'd promised to go. But when she'd looked over the sign-in sheet from the event this morning, Mr. Martin's name wasn't on it.

She pulled into the older man's driveway and saw the neglected yard and house. The bad feeling in the pit of her stomach grew. Madi got out of her car, grabbed the bag of groceries she'd picked up for him and knocked at the front door.

No one answered.

Madi tried again, but something felt off. She wriggled the handle and the door opened. "Mr. Martin?" she called. "It's me, Madison Scott."

"Go away!" a feeble, yet somehow still arrogant, voice called.

Ignoring the command, Madi walked inside the dark house, flipped on the lights and saw Mr. Martin sprawled on the wooden floor at the base of a set of stairs. She dropped everything and rushed to the older man's side. "You got dizzy and fell down the stairs?"

"No, I like to nap here," Mr. Martin snapped. "I told you to go away. You have no right to be here."

Okay, so at least he was conscious, with no obvious disorientation. Probably vasovagal syncope then. Madi checked his limbs quickly and found nothing obviously broken. "Can you stand?"

"Sure. I just chose to be the rug today. Why the hell are you here? Don't you ever get tired of saving people?"

"And miss your charming wit and sweet nature?" Madi retorted. "Never. Can you sit up for me?"

Mr. Martin slapped Madi's hands away but didn't move.

Question answered. Madi sat on the floor next to him as she called an ambulance, then rifled through the bag of groceries she'd brought. "While we wait for the EMTs to arrive, how about a snack? I bought soup, or I could make you a sandwich, or—"

"Go away! I'm old. I'm alone. I'm going to die any second now. Just *let me*. Why did you have to call the EMS? Do you have any idea how expensive that is?"

"I do. And I called because you need help. I can't move you myself. Also, you're not that old," Madi said. "You're just mean. And *that's* why you're alone. You could have friends if you'd stop snapping at everyone. Lucille would take you into her posse in an instant if you were even the slightest bit less evil. She *loves* snark."

"I'm *alone*."

"You have me," Madi said. She pulled out a kid's box of apple juice and shoved the attached straw through the foil-covered hole in the front. "Here. Drink this. It's your favorite."

"Not thirsty."

"Then how about I make you some chicken soup?"

A slight spark of life came into Mr. Martin's eyes. "Is it from a can?"

"No," Madi said, her tone dripping with sarcasm. "I spent all day cooking it myself. After raising the chickens and growing the carrots and celery in my garden. What do you think?"

The older man sniffed disdainfully. "I don't eat food from a can."

"Fine." Madi pulled out a bag of prunes as sirens wailed in the distance.

He snatched it from her and opened it with shaking fingers.

Madi smiled.

"You're enjoying my misery?"

"I knew I'd get you with the prunes."

After a minute or two, with the sugar in his system, Mr. Martin glared as the ambulance pulled up in the driveway. "I'd have been fine without you."

"Sure. You'd be even better if you took care of yourself."

"What do you know? You're not taking care of yourself either."

"What does that mean?"

"The *boyfriend.*" He said the last word like a curse. Mr. Martin gave her a snide stare as the ambulance crew, including Tate of course, rushed inside with their medical packs and gear. Tate looked at Mr. Martin, then Madi, a brow raised. Mr. Martin continued. "Yes, I heard about you two at the auction."

Good Lord.

While Madi prepped the older man's arm to insert an IV, Tate checked his vitals, not missing a beat as he said, "I'm not her boyfriend."

Madi bit her lip and cleaned up the mess she'd made when she'd dropped the bag of groceries.

Mr. Martin sneered at her. "So, you're giving away the milk for free then?"

"First of all, I'm not a cow," Madi snapped back. "And second of all, we're *not* discussing this."

"Vitals good. BP's normal, O2 sats normal, pulse good," Tate said, slinging his stethoscope back around his neck. "Do you have pain anywhere, Mr. Martin?"

"Besides my butt from dealing with you people?" the older man growled. "Leave me alone! Ow!"

"Can't do that, Mr. Martin," Tate said. "IV in.

Let me put on a cervical brace just in case, then we'll get him on the gurney."

"I don't want a brace or a gurney! Which part of 'get out' don't you people understand?"

When no one responded to his nastiness, Mr. Martin seemed to refocus his efforts on Madi as Tate put on his neck brace. Then together with his EMT partner, Tate hoisted the man up and onto the gurney they'd rolled into the room when they came in. Mr. Martin narrowed his gaze on Madi as he was buckled in. "I know what you're trying to do, missy," he snarled, his gaze darting to Tate, then returning to Madi. "You're trying to save him. Like you try to save everyone. But even you must realize he isn't interested in settling down with a small-town nurse, not for the long term."

The jab hit a little close to home because it was true.

Am I trying to save him? Because I couldn't save Karrie?

"Watch it," Madi said, deflecting. "Or the prunes stay with me."

"Hmph."

It took a few more minutes for Tate and the other EMT to roll Mr. Martin out to the ambulance. Madi followed them to the door. The older man's vitals were stronger now, which was good because Lucille, who'd apparently walked up from Sunny Village a few doors down, joined them.

The elderly woman stepped inside the rig, her eyes on Mr. Martin. "Luther, are you all right?"

The oddest thing happened. Right before Madi's eyes, Mr. Martin seemed to soften a bit. Even... *smile*. Or at least that's what Madi thought the baring of his teeth meant.

Mr. Martin flushed and looked away. "I'm fine."

"Liar." Lucille moved in beside his gurney. "You get dizzy again?"

"Of course not."

"Luther?"

"Maybe a little," Mr. Martin said sheepishly. "But only for a minute."

Lucille nodded to Madi. "I'm glad you checked on him then. He doesn't make it easy I know. But we take care of our own here in Wyckford, even the prickly ones."

Madi smiled, knowing Lucille was right. Then she gave Mr. Martin a pointed stare. "It's good to know he's not *alone*."

The older man rolled his eyes, but shockingly not a single mean thing crossed his lips.

Lucille had on a neon green tracksuit that clashed horribly with her pink lipstick and her black-and-yellow tennis shoes. Madi practically needed sunglasses to look at her.

Mr. Martin narrowed his gaze. "You can leave, Lucille. These people insist on taking me to the hospital."

"Then I'm coming too." Lucille smiled.

Tate gave Madi one last unreadable look as he closed the doors on the rig. Then they took off, lights and sirens going.

Madi went home and unlocked her front door. She glanced at the little foyer desk—where she and Tate had made love—and sighed.

Meow.

"I hear you." She fed Violet, then glared at her foyer desk, telling it, "This is your fault."

The table had nothing to say in its defense.

She ached for Tate with her whole mind and body.

Madi showered and changed, then headed over to the Buzzy Bird, needing an immediate infusion of chocolate cake. As she entered the diner, the comforting sounds of people talking and laughing washed over her, and her stomach growled.

With everything that had happened with Mr. Martin, she'd missed dinner. Cassie was there too, alone. Madi knew Brock was working a shift in the ER that night. She slipped into the booth and eyed the empty spot on the table in front of her. "You not eating?"

"Nah. I'll eat with Brock later," Cassie said, her cheeks pink.

Madi's teeth ached. She was so happy for her friend and so sad for herself. She'd made a horrible mess of things with Tate.

Then Luna appeared, holding a slice of cake so dark it was almost black, and three forks.

"Five customers have already tried to buy this from me, so you're welcome." After locking the door, Luna returned and sat with a sigh. "God, it feels good to get off my feet. This day has been nuts. They repaired all the damage from the storm, but now the sprinkler system in here has been acting wonky. The men have been out a couple times to look at it, but so far, they haven't pinpointed the problem yet. Like strange noises from the pipes and stuff. It's weird."

Madi didn't respond. She was still too busy stuffing her face.

Luna frowned at her. "What's wrong?"

"Nothing." Madi shrugged.

Not letting her off the hook that easy, Luna continued to push. "Something's wrong. I can tell."

Cassie sipped her water, then asked Madi, "Trouble in paradise?"

"No." She finally set her fork down, unable to eat another bite. "Tate and I… It was just fun. That's all."

"Really?" Cassie asked. "Because it looked like more than fun to me."

Madi sighed, then shook her head. "I don't want to talk about it."

"But we *do*." Luna smiled. "C'mon. Maybe we can help."

"It was a fling. That's all. That's what we agreed

on from the start. But then I took it too far…" She bit her bottom lip. "You guys know I'm not hardwired for that. I like strong and stable. But there's something about Tate. I know he's leaving. I know this thing between us is only temporary. But every time we are together, I want…" She closed her eyes. "More."

"Sweetie." Cassie squeezed Madi's hand.

Luna put an arm around Madi. "I'm so sorry. I tried to tell you."

Madi slumped forward. "I know. And I appreciate that. I do. I tried to follow your advice, but I couldn't keep things light. I tried, but… I think I love him and he's leaving and—"

Someone knocked on the door.

Madi looked over to see Tate and her traitorous heart clutched at the sight of him.

Their gazes held for an unfathomably long beat, and as always, she got a little thrill. He always seemed bigger than life, and a whole lot more than she could handle. Especially in his EMT uniform. But there was something different about him now. He looked weary and a little rough around the edges.

She loved him. And she missed him. Even though it had only been a few hours since they'd seen each other. Madi wanted to kiss away his problems. Hold him.

It made no sense because he was leaving. He'd been up-front and honest about that with her. And he'd take a big piece of her heart along with him when he went, but it was a done deal. Madi also knew she wanted whatever he had to give her in the meantime. Because with him, she wasn't Miss Goody Two-Shoes. She wasn't always thinking, planning, overseeing.

With Tate, she was just…*alive*.

He smiled, touching a finger to the glass.

"Sorry." Madi slid out of the booth, ignoring her gaping friends. "I have to go."

Outside, the stars were bright, like scattered diamonds on the velvet night sky. The waves from Buzzards Bay lapped against the shore in the distance. They walked along the pier in the chilly air, past the dark arcade and the closed shops. Past everything until there was nothing but emptiness and water ahead.

Madi stopped and leaned over the railing facing the bay. "I'm sorry about earlier," she said quietly. "Mr. Martin can be super mean." She sighed. "And I'm also sorry for seconding your name for that job without asking you first. I had no right to do that."

When Tate didn't answer, Madi searched his face in the shadows, hoping for understanding. Forgiveness. Or at the very least, a sign that he'd heard her.

She got nothing, and her heart sank.

After a minute, he leaned on the railing beside her to stare out at the water. "You said before you didn't understand my situation, why I am the way I am, because I never explained it to you. So, I want to tell you now." He took a deep breath before continuing. "After the accident, I was a mess. Saving lives is my job, it's my life. It's who I am. But after what happened with my team, I don't trust myself. Not completely."

She placed a hand on his arm. "Tate…"

"No. That night in the helicopter…" He hesitated. "It was my fault. Those people died because of my bad decision. I can't ever change that. I can't ever atone for it."

Madi waited a few beats, letting his words hang in the air, then drift away with the tide. "Tate, you may not want to hear this, but you're smart and strong and kind and generous. You protect people. You heal people. That's who you are. I trust you with my life. You don't have anything to atone for. That accident wasn't your fault."

He was quiet, seemingly absorbing that, then he turned to her and ran a finger over the infinity charm around her neck, looking at it in the moonlight. "I've spent the last four years believing that I didn't deserve comfort. Punishing myself, trying to pay for what I'd done." He let out a breath and dropped his hand from her. "I didn't want anyone close. Because I *can't* protect the people I care for, Madi. I tried with my team, with those victims in the ocean, and I failed."

She couldn't imagine what losing his team,

his friends, the people he'd been sent to rescue must've been like for him, trapped out in the ocean, hurt and alone, grieving and helpless.

Or maybe she could. She'd felt much the same after she'd lost Karrie.

Madi held the charm in her hand and closed her eyes for a minute and pictured her sister's laughing eyes. "My sister gave me this the night she died. She told me we'd be forever connected because of it. She wore it all the time, and I always used to bug her to let me borrow it. I wanted to be just like her. It used to drive her nuts. Then, that last night, Karrie came to my room. She kissed my cheek and told me to be good, that being good would keep me out of trouble. She made me promise. Then she said she'd watch over me, guide my way, make sure I was okay." Her throat tightened painfully. "The next day they found her body."

Tate pulled Madi against him. She fisted her hands in his shirt as she cried. She was supposed to be comforting him here, but she was the one breaking down.

"I know you're hurting, but you're not alone, Tate," Madi managed to choke out against his chest. "And you're not responsible for the death of your team or the victims. You were in a terrible situation, and they made their choices. Please stop punishing yourself."

* * *

They stood like that, locked together, a light breeze blowing her hair around. A strand of it clung to the stubble on his jaw and Tate left it there, bound to her.

"How's Mr. Martin?" Madi asked at last.

"Doing well when I checked before leaving after my shift," Tate said.

He'd left a message at the Air Force recruitment office, but hadn't gotten a call back yet.

Madi finally lifted her head and looked at him. "I'm glad you're still here."

He held her gaze, his own steady. "For now." Then Tate pressed his forehead to hers. "You should walk away from me right now and avoid any more heartbreak. I'm not worth it. You deserve better."

Instead, she pushed him up against the railing and kissed him. Took full advantage of his surprise, opening her mouth over his, causing a rush of heat and the melting of all his bones. In less than a single heartbeat, Madi had stolen his breath and his heart.

"If the decision is mine to make," she said breathing hard, her voice utterly serious once she'd pulled back, "then I'm staying with you, for as long as I can have you."

CHAPTER EIGHTEEN

THE NEXT MORNING, Tate woke with a gloriously naked Madi sprawled over the top of him. He'd always valued his own space. He was a big guy and didn't like to feel crowded. Madi was half his size, and as it turned out, a bed hog. She was also a blanket hog and a pillow hog.

But that was okay. They'd made love again the night before, both knowing what this was and wasn't. Then they'd fallen asleep together. Didn't mean anything. If it happened again…well, *then* he'd panic. "Madi."

She snored softly, and his heart squeezed.

"Are you working today?"

He had one hand on her butt and squeezed lightly. She froze and jerked upright. "What time is it?"

"Seven." Tate nuzzled his face in her crazy hair.

"*Seven?*" Madi leapt out of the bed, frantically searching for her clothes.

Enjoying the show, Tate leaned back, hands behind his head, as he grinned.

"Where are my panties?" she demanded.

"Under the chair."

She reached for them, giving him an amazing view that made him groan.

"Not here!" she yelled; her voice muffled from her position.

"No? Check beneath my jeans then," he said.

She straightened, blowing the hair out of her face, her gaze narrowed on him.

He smiled.

She crawled there, another hot view, and snatched her panties, then disappeared into the bathroom. Five minutes later she reappeared, freshly showered and dressed, looking thoroughly flustered.

"Come here," he said, waggling his fingers at her.

"No. If I come over there, we'll never get out of this bedroom."

"True." He laughed, feeling lighthearted and… *happy*. "I want to put my mouth on your—"

"Stop." She shook her head and grabbed her keys, her still-wet hair pulled back into a sloppy braid. "I have to go!"

"Come on," he said. "It'll be the best part of your day, I promise."

She hesitated, biting her lower lip, looking tempted, then rushed to the door. "Bye."

Tate stayed there for a while after Madi left. Then his phone beeped. Rolling out of bed, he accessed his messages and saw one from the recruitment office. That one could wait for later. The next was from Mr. Ryan.

"Hey, man," the vet said. That was it, the full extent of the message. It could mean anything from "let's have dinner" to "I'm jonesing for a fix and need someone to talk to."

There were two others as well. One from Mark looking for a gym partner and another from Brock asking if he'd given any more thought to the flight crew job.

Tate stared at his phone, realizing that while he'd been busy trying to keep to himself in this slow-paced, sleepy little town he'd made ties to people, connections he hadn't known were there.

He got up and showered, then got dressed. After running some errands, he called in to the ambulance service for his updated schedule, then worked on the Chevelle for a while. By the time he was done in the garage, it was past dinner time. Too late to call back the recruitment office, so he drove into Wyckford, thinking he'd stop by and see Mr. Ryan at the halfway house and take food from the café. But as he passed the hospital, he saw Madi through the glass and before he knew what he was doing, he'd pulled into the lot and parked. Tate got out of the Chevelle and walked into the empty clinic lobby. From the hallway, he heard voices from the open exam room door— Madi talking to whoever was in there with her.

From outside, he'd seen her purple scrubs. It

was a good color for her. Her hair was still in the braid, but a few strands had escaped over the hours they'd been apart. He inched down the hall a bit more to get a better look at her. She wasn't good at hiding her feelings, and right now she looked on edge, tired and frustrated.

A long day, no doubt made longer because they'd spent most of the night tearing up his sheets. Tate still couldn't say he regretted it, and he knew exactly what he'd do to relax her, but he had to remind himself she wasn't his to take care of. By his own choice.

Once he talked to the recruitment office and his reenlistment paperwork was filed, he'd be out of Wyckford in no time. Then Madi would stay up all night with someone else. Someone who'd take care of her, help her unwind at the end of the day. Someone not him.

And whoever she chose, he had nothing to say about it, because it was none of his business.

But it still sucked.

"Just trust me," she was saying to the patient in the room with her, pulling a set of keys from her pocket and opening the medicine cabinet, eyeing the samples there before grabbing a box. "Take these. One a day."

"What are you poisoning me with now?" the man asked. Tate recognized his voice. Mr. Martin.

"Vitamins," Madi said.

Mr. Martin took the samples. "Vitamins are

a sham. A way for the drug companies to make money off us unsuspecting idiots."

She crossed her arms. "Your bloodwork after your fall shows you're anemic. These will help. Or you can keep passing out and waiting until EMS finds you on the floor again. Your choice."

A long silence followed. Then Mr. Martin said, "You used to be afraid of me. You used to tremble like a child."

"Things change." Madi's tone was mild. No judgment, no recriminations. "Take the vitamins. Don't make me come over every night and make you take them."

"Well, if you're going to out-mean me."

"I am," Madi said firmly. "I don't want to be mean to you, but if that's what it takes for you to take care of yourself, then that's what I'll do."

Turning from Mr. Martin, Madi caught sight of Tate standing there. Her surprised smile only added to the ache inside him, but he nodded and stepped back, leaning against the wall to wait.

She looked at her patient once more. "I have something else for you—hold on." She came out into the hall, shutting the door behind her. She flashed Tate another smile, then vanished into the next room. When she returned, Madi handed Mr. Martin a flyer before guiding him from the clinic.

A few minutes later she returned to Tate. "Hey."

"Hey." He hiked his chin toward the lobby. "You should lock the front door when you're alone."

"I wasn't alone, and this is Wyckford. I'm as safe as it gets."

"Not with that medicine cabinet you're not. Someone could break in. Someone desperate."

"It's only temporary. We're getting a much better setup next week." She smiled, still not taking her safety seriously enough for Tate. "What brings you here?"

"I was on my way to see Mr. Ryan," he said. "Are you done for the night?"

"I am."

"Good. Then I'm going to collect on a favor."

Madi sputtered, then laughed. "What exactly *is* this favor?"

He pushed off the wall and came toward her. "I need the same thing you needed the night of the auction. A date."

"To the halfway house?"

"No. I just remembered I have other plans tonight." He brought her hand to his mouth, brushing his lips against her palm as he watched her over their joined fingers. "Say yes, Madi."

Staring at him, she cupped his face. "Always."

His heart rolled, exposing its underbelly. He was equipped to deal with emergencies, to serve. Not to love.

Never to love.

Madi had no idea what his plans were. Tate had made some phone calls before they'd left the clinic, but she hadn't been able to hear anything and he wouldn't tell her where they were going. Now on the highway, heading toward Boston. Once there, he drove to a block lined with designer boutiques and parked.

He pulled her out of the car and into a dress shop. "Something for the theater," he said to the pretty saleswoman who came forward. Then he turned to Madi. "Whatever you want."

Confused, she asked, "Whatever I want? I don't even know what we're doing here."

"The night on the town package from the auction. Tonight's the last night of the orchestra. I thought you could use a night off." He looked endearingly baffled. "Don't women like romantic surprises?" For the first time since Madi had known him, Tate looked uncomfortable in his own skin. "You're right. This was a stupid idea. Let's go get a pizza and beer. Whatever you want."

Madi knew he was far more at ease in the role of tough guy than romance guy and he'd probably certainly have preferred pizza and beer over the orchestra. And yet he'd thought of her. He'd wanted to give her a night off, even if it was last minute, and he'd brought her to a place filled with gorgeous, designer clothes so she wouldn't stress about what to wear. Madi also knew, deep down, that this was goodbye. But she wanted this. With him. She went on tiptoe to whisper, "Thank you."

Tate claimed her mouth in one quick, hot kiss. "Take your time. I'll be waiting."

He walked out the front door and drove away in the Chevelle.

She stared after him. "That man is crazy."

"Crazy *fine*," the salesclerk murmured, then gestured around them. "What would you like to try on?"

Thirty minutes later, Madi was decked out in a silky siren-red dress that made her feel like a sex kitten. She tried to see the price tag, but the clerk had hidden it. "He said you weren't allowed to look at the prices."

Good Lord.

By the time Madi exited the shop, she felt like Cinderella. And her prince stepped out of the Chevelle to greet her in a well-fitted, expensive tux that nearly made her trip over her new strappy high heels. She'd seen Tate in a suit before at the auction. Since then, she'd seen him in jeans, in his uniform and in nothing at all. He always looked mouthwateringly gorgeous. But tonight… "Wow."

He took her hand and pulled her in. "You take my breath away."

That's when Madi realized he was looking at her differently. Heart-stoppingly so.

Dinner was at a French restaurant so amazing she started to regret not going one size up on the dress. But the wine quickly reduced any lingering anxiety. The problem was, combined with a long day at work and almost no sleep the night before, her eyes were drooping by the time they got to the orchestra. Still, she accepted another glass of Zinfandel as they found their seats. The curtain went up.

And that's the last thing Madi remembered.

When she woke, the theater was quiet, and Tate leaned over her with an amused smile.

"What?" She blinked, confused.

His smile spread to a grin. "You snore."

"Do not!" She straightened, staring at the empty stage and the few people left around them. "It's over? I missed the whole thing?"

He pulled her to her feet. "That's okay. You didn't miss the best part."

"What's that?"

"Wait for it." He drove them home and after they walked into her house, Tate slowly stripped Madi out of her new dress and bra and panties, groaning at the sight of her in just the heels.

"You are the most beautiful woman I've ever seen." He carried her to the bed. "I know how tired you are, so let me take care of you for a change."

"I'm not tired," she said. "I took a very nice nap at the orchestra."

With a soft laugh, he crawled up her body, kissing and nipping as he went. "I'm offering to do all the work here. And I'm ready for the best part."

"What's that?" she panted against his cheek.

He gently bit her lower lip and tugged, then

soothed the ache with his tongue, making every single nerve ending in her body beg for more. "You. You're the best part."

Her heart caught. "Me?"

"Always," he breathed, then set about proving it.

CHAPTER NINETEEN

THE NEXT AFTERNOON, Madi was in the ER doing her damnedest not to dwell on the fact Tate would probably be leaving town soon. She was just checking in a patient who'd been brought in after breaking up a fight when a call came in from Camilla.

"I'm at the clinic," the young nurse said. "And we have a problem."

She finished up with her patient, then hurried over to the old west wing. "What's wrong?"

Camilla showed her the medicine lockup. "Four boxes of OxyContin are missing."

Madi's heart sank. "What?"

"A month's supply."

"What?" She stared at the cabinet in shock.

"Yeah. I was just closing after the teen advocacy meeting when I found it like this. I called Judith already." Camilla looked a bit sheepish. "I didn't want to cause problems for you, but I also didn't want to not report it, then have it come out later and for anyone to think I tried to cover it up. I never even got into the lockup today at all."

"No. It's fine. You did the right thing." Madi nodded even as her mind raced. If Camilla hadn't been in the lockup today, that meant the last person in there had been Madi yesterday when *she'd* been in charge. She remembered getting into the locked storage cabinet several times for different patients—once for birth control samples and another time for smoker's patches. And then for Mr. Martin's vitamins. A tight feeling spread through her chest. There were only two reasons to take OxyContin.

To sell or to use. Stealing them was an act of desperation, and addicts were desperate.

Karrie had been desperate too, and Madi had failed her.

Who else am I failing now?

She returned to the ER heartsick and found herself almost immediately summoned to Bud Lofton's office. When she arrived, several board members were there, including Judith and her mother, waiting.

"How could this have happened?" Bud asked, his tone stern.

Madi took a deep breath. "We received samples early yesterday for the weekend health clinic, as usual. I stocked the cabinet myself and locked it afterward."

"Exactly how much is missing?" Judith asked.

She had to have already known. Camilla had told her she'd called their boss and reported it.

"Four boxes. Each one is a week's supply. So, a month total."

She'd gone over the inventory a hundred times in her head, hoping she'd just miscalculated.

She hadn't.

Someone had stolen those meds from right under Madi's nose. An anguished, distraught, frantic act, by a person she most likely knew by name because everyone knew everyone else in Wyckford.

"We'll need a list of who came through the clinic yesterday for the police," Bud said.

This was what she'd dreaded. "But the patient rosters for the clinic are supposed to be anonymous."

"I know, but this is out of our hands now. I'm sorry," Judith said. "The list, Madison. By tomorrow morning at the latest."

"Please. I can fix this," Madi begged. "Let me—"

"The only way to fix this now is by trusting the police to do their jobs," Bud said. "This is a legal matter now. A felony has been committed and that puts the entire hospital under a huge burden of liability. Understand?"

"Of course. But—"

"No buts, Madi." Bud cut her off. "Don't put your job on the line as well by making this more difficult."

Her heart lurched, and she ground her teeth to avoid saying something she'd regret later.

"And until this is resolved," Judith added, looking regretful, "the clinic stays closed."

Another stab to Madi's gut. "Understood."

Somehow, she managed to get through the rest of her shift. All she wanted to do was get home and be alone, but her mother caught her in the parking lot. "What's going on here?"

Madi frowned. "What do you mean?"

"Honey, you're the most conscientious person I know. I don't believe for a second that you don't have some idea of who's behind this. Why won't you tell them?"

"Mom, I honestly don't know who took those drugs. Your guess is as good as mine. I just want to leave now, okay?"

Her mother looked deep into Madi's eyes, then shook her head. "Madi, this isn't your fault."

"Really?" She pulled free and opened her car door. "Because the hospital board seems to think it is. Someone has to take the fall, and since I'm in charge of the clinic, I guess that person will be me."

"Unless you can find out who took the pills."

Exhaustion took over and Madi slammed the door, then leaned back against it, all the emotions she'd buried earlier rushing to the surface and overwhelming her. "I don't know what happened yesterday, but it *was* my fault. The board is right. I allowed that to happen on my watch. But what bothers me even more is the fact that someone I know is in trouble and I can't help them." A sob choked her, shutting off her words, and Madi slapped a hand over her mouth. "I hate feeling helpless like this. It reminds me of what happened to Karrie. I didn't know she was floundering so badly, Mom. How did I not know?"

"Oh, honey," her mother said, pulling Madi into a hug. "You should have talked to me about this. None of what happened with Karrie was your fault. None."

Madi buried her face against her mother's shoulder. "I just keep thinking that if I'd cared more, done more, she wouldn't have…"

"Honey, listen to me," her mother said fiercely, pulling back to look in Madi's eyes. "You were sixteen. None of what happened was your fault. It wasn't anyone's fault. It took me a lot of years and heartache to realize that and if I can save you the same trouble I will. You are not responsible for other people's actions, Madi. Understand?"

Madi let out a shaky breath. "But I still feel like I failed her. And now with this situation, I don't want to make the same mistake, Mom. I can't let anyone else fall through the cracks like she did. That's why I work so hard. That's why I started the clinic. To help people like Karrie. To make up for not being able to save her."

Her mother pulled her close again and whispered against the top of Madi's head, "Sometimes people must do for themselves. Find their own will, their own happy. Their own path. You can support them with that, but you can't do it for them, honey. You know that."

Madi sniffled in response. She *did* know that, deep down. She'd just forgotten with everything that had happened. And regardless of why she'd started the clinic, it was a part of her now. A vital one she wanted to keep going. She pulled back and gave her mother a weepy smile. "Thanks for the pep talk, Mom. But I'm willing to fight for the clinic and whoever took those drugs because they need help. That was a desperate act, not a malicious one. This is my hill to die on."

A beat or two passed before her mother gave a reluctant nod of understanding.

Afterward, Madi got into her car and drove straight to Tate's house.

He didn't answer her knock. The place was quiet. Empty. She put a hand to her chest, knowing last night had been a goodbye. For a minute, she panicked. Would he really disappear without a word?

Frustrated and annoyed, mainly with herself, she went home, intending to get into bed and tug the covers over her head and have a good, long cry. She dropped her keys on the foyer table, then kicked off her shoes in the hallway and walked into her bedroom as she struggled to pull her scrub top off over her head. But it caught in her hair and pulled painfully. "Dammit!"

She stood there arms up, face covered by scrubs, when two strong arms enveloped her.

Madi gave a startled scream before she was gathered against a familiar warm, hard chest. "Tate?"

He chuckled. "Expecting someone else?"

"I wasn't expecting anyone at all. Please help me get this shirt off."

Instead, he slid a thigh between hers.

"*Tate*…" She squirmed and only succeeded in getting herself tangling up more and cursing a blue streak as a result.

Laughing, Tate finally freed her from the offending garment and tossed it over his head while still pressing her against the door. "Where'd you learn such filthy words?"

"Just because I live in a small town doesn't mean I'm sheltered," Madi said, not in the mood to play.

"Got it." His voice sounded dark and edgy tonight. Apparently, he wasn't feeling playful either. A chord of need struck deep inside her despite the awful day. "I've been looking for you."

Her heart yearned to let him take all her worries and woes away. In the back of her mind, an image of that empty Vicodin bottle from his pocket flashed before she dismissed it entirely. Tate wouldn't do that to her. He was a paramedic.

A medical professional just like her. Never mind the statistics that said ten to fifteen percent of health-care professionals would abuse drugs in their lifetimes. Tate was a good man, an honorable man. He'd been clean for three years. Yes, he'd been through tough times recently, but hadn't they all? He wouldn't do it. Didn't do it. She believed that to the bottom of her soul.

They could discuss it later. Right now, their time together was limited. Too limited. Between kisses, she said, "I want you."

In the shadows, his eyes gleamed with heat and intent. She kissed him again, swallowing his rough groan, savoring the taste of him, done with waiting. "My bed. Now."

They staggered farther into the room and fell onto her mattress.

"Take the rest off too," he demanded right back in that quiet voice that made Madi go weak in the knees. She unhooked her bra and wriggled out of her panties, then got distracted by watching him strip. Tate tugged his EMS uniform shirt over his head. His hands went to his fly, his movements quick and economical as he bared his gorgeous body. In two seconds, he was naked, one hundred percent of his attention completely fixed on her as he put on a condom. And apparently, she was moving too slowly because he took over, wrapping his fingers around each of her ankles, giving a hard tug so she fell flat on her back. He was on her in a heartbeat. "All day while I was working, all I could see was you."

She slid her hands down his sinewy, cut torso, planning on licking that same path as soon as she got a chance. "Yeah?"

"Oh, yeah," he said silkily. "You've had me in a state all day, Madison Scott."

The air crackled with electricity, and he kissed her again. His touch as demanding as his mouth, his hands finding her breasts, teasing her nipples, sliding between her legs. She was ready for him. He groaned and pushed inside her with one hard thrust. "You feel amazing."

Madi felt him to the depths of her soul. She wrapped her arms around his broad shoulders and melted into the hard planes of his body. Emotion welled within her, and she bit her lip closed to hold in the words that wanted to escape.

She stared up into his eyes, her heart aching. His hands slid up to her hips, positioning her exactly as he wanted. Wrapping her legs around his waist, she whispered his name, needing him to move.

His fingers skimmed her spine, leaving a trail of heat she felt all the way to her toes, taking her exactly where she needed to go without words. And that was the point of no return for her. Tate was what she wanted, what she'd never had the nerve to reach out and grasp for herself before. He didn't want her to depend on him, and yet he'd given her the security to be who she was. If only he'd stay.

It wouldn't happen, she knew. So, she had to settle for this, for the right now.

Sometime in the night, Tate woke up wrapped in warm woman. He had one hand entangled in Madi's crazy hair, the other on her bare butt, holding her possessively to him.

Jesus.

If he stayed with her tonight, it would be a mistake, and Tate didn't make mistakes, much less the same one twice. With more effort than it should have taken, he finally managed to get out of bed without waking her. Gathered his things, he left her, quietly shutting the door behind him.

In the hallway, he dumped his stuff on the floor and started dressing, hesitating once to look back at the door. He wanted to go back in there.

Don't do it, man.

He reached for his shirt and realized it wasn't there and he also only had one sock. He stubbed his toe on his own shoe and swore softly, then kicked the thing down the hall.

Tate froze when the bedroom door opened, and the light came on.

Madi blinked sleepily at him, tousled and adorable wearing nothing but his missing shirt. "Everything okay?"

"Sorry. Didn't mean to wake you."

"Are you leaving?"

"Yeah, I… I'm going." He needed to. Before he couldn't leave Wyckford at all.

She looked down at his lone sock, the things that had spilled out of his pants pockets he hadn't picked up yet—his keys, his wallet, the empty Vicodin bottle.

She bent and picked that up, staring at the label on the meds for a long time—the three-year-old date of the prescription, the refills available to him which he'd never used. Finally, she handed the bottle back to him with a gentle smile. "Stay. Just tonight."

He couldn't. "Madi—"

But she covered his mouth with her fingers, took his hand, and drew him back into her bedroom, into her bed and into her warm, soft heart.

CHAPTER TWENTY

THE NEXT MORNING Tate and Mark went for a hike after the gym. They walked a well-worn trail until they reached a plateau about the size of a football field, with a decent view of Buzzards Bay in the distance.

"Good spot," Tate said.

"Lot of stupid teenagers come here." Mark shrugged. "Four-wheeling in Daddy's truck or messing around. Then they get lost, and we rescue them. Still beats fighting a fire in Chicago in high summer in full tactical gear though." He laughed, then stared out at the horizon. "You hear what happened at the clinic?"

Tate frowned.

"Someone stole Oxy samples from the locked cabinet."

Tate's gut tightened, remembering how Madi had studied the empty Vicodin bottle that had fallen out of his pocket. "When?"

Mark watched him carefully. "Not sure, but probably the night before. Police are still investigating."

The night he'd taken Madi to the orchestra. Which meant she'd known last night and hadn't said a word to him about it. He tried to think of a reason she wouldn't have mentioned the missing meds that didn't involve her thinking it was him but couldn't. Tate forced words past his constricted throat. "Is she in trouble?"

"The clinic's closed down until the cops find the perpetrator. And depending on what they find, it might stay that way. Madi accepted the blame, of course."

"How do you know all of this?"

"Because I'm the fire department rep on the hospital board." Mark eyed him. "Law enforcement wants a list of patients there on the day the pills went missing. Madi objected because the clinic's services are supposed to be anonymous. But the board wasn't happy with her decision, which puts her job as an ER nurse at risk too."

Christ. Tate let out a breath and closed his eyes. "I was there that night. At the HSC." He looked at Mark, then pulled out his phone only to see no bars of reception. "I need to go."

Without waiting to see if his friend followed, Tate started back down the trail toward his house. He needed to see Madi. Halfway home, he finally got a decent signal and dialed her number. She didn't answer.

Mark called to him from farther back. "I know where she is."

Tate looked back at him.

"At the diner with Luna and Cassie. I was there earlier because their sprinkler system was acting up again," Mark said. "Should be fine for now, but eventually they need to replace it."

They reached Tate's house and rather than going inside, he went directly to the garage and grabbed the keys to the Chevelle, climbing behind the wheel while Mark slid in the passenger side. They took off in a squeal of tires, heading for town.

A few minutes later, they parked in the Buzzy Bird's lot. The place was decorated for Thanksgiving with papier-mâché turkeys and pilgrim hats hanging from the ceiling tiles and streamers around the windows. It didn't match the fifties decor but was definitely eye-popping.

The noise level was high from the full breakfast crowd. Tate recognized most of the faces now, which meant he'd been there far too long. Madi was at the counter, and he sidled past a small group of people waiting to be seated. Cassie sat beside her, and Luna stood behind the counter from them. As Tate got closer, he heard Luna ask, "What did your boss say when you quit?"

Oh, God.

"Not much really." Madi shrugged. "They were going to have to fire me anyway. Bud had no choice, so I just saved them the trouble."

"Wow," Cassie said. "I'm so sorry all this happened."

Madi let out a combination laugh-sob. "Me too."

"What are your plans now?" Luna asked. "We can always use more help around here, if you need something to keep you busy until you get another nursing job."

"I'm thinking I'll work for a quiet little doctor's office somewhere and forget about all this." Madi shook her head. "I don't want to talk about it right now, okay?"

Tate moved in beside Madi. "You'd wither up and die of boredom in a quiet little doctor's office."

Madi whirled on her stool to stare up at him, her eyes shining with unshed tears. Everyone in the diner froze, watching them. Except Luna, who stared at Mark as he took a seat at the counter to watch the circus.

Tate narrowed his eyes at all the nosy folks of Wyckford. No one took the hint. His glare used to terrorize people. But it hadn't worked for him in this town, not once. Giving up, he looked at Madi again. "Why didn't you tell me about the missing drugs?"

"Because I know that you didn't take them." Madi said.

"Excuse me," Lucille said from a nearby table. "Did someone take medicine from the clinic?"

Madi pinched the bridge of her nose. "Which part of private matter don't you understand, Lucille?"

The older woman blinked at her, apparently astonished. "Are you sassing me, Madison Scott?"

"No." Madi grimaced, then added politely, "But stay out of my business, *please*."

"All you had to do was ask, dear." Lucille smiled. "And I'm glad to see your backbone emerging. Looks great on you."

Madi stared at the older woman, then back at Tate who'd been rendered speechless.

Because I know you didn't take them.

Somehow, despite his best efforts, Madi knew him, inside and out, and accepted him. Faults and failures and all. And she'd believed in him, no questions asked.

This didn't really help now though since someone *had* taken the meds under her watch.

Tate could tell by looking at her that she *knew* who the responsible party was but didn't want to say. Even now she was still trying to save people. "If you know I didn't take the pills, then why didn't you turn over the list of people at the clinic to the police?"

Madi's temper ignited in her eyes. She stood and poked him in the chest with her finger, her cheeks flushed. "Because maybe you're not the only person I care about around here."

She still had on purple scrubs with a long-sleeved T-shirt beneath—*his* shirt if he wasn't mistaken. There was a mysterious lump of things in her pockets, and a red heart drawn on one of her white tennis shoes. Her hair was completely out of control, as usual, and she seemed ready to take down anyone who got in her path. She'd never looked more beautiful to him.

"Madi," Tate said, knowing how much her work meant to her. How much the clinic meant to her. How much Wyckford meant to her. "You quit your job."

In that moment, he made his decision. He'd take the fall, for her. He'd failed to save the people he cared for once before. He refused to fail again. "It's my fault," he said loud enough for all the eavesdroppers to hear. "I took advantage of you, Madi."

Two stools over, Mark groaned and shook his head. "Aw, man. Don't do it."

Madi scowled. "What are you doing?"

"Telling these folks what happened with the missing meds at the clinic," he said carefully.

"Hold it!" Mr. Martin moved in, jabbing his cane toward Tate. "Yeah, I'm talking to you, punk."

Punk? Tate stood a foot and a half taller than the old man and outweighed him by at least a hundred pounds. He stared down at Mr. Martin in shock.

Mark laughed. "Punk. I like it."

It'd been a long time since anyone had gotten

in Tate's face, even longer since he'd been called a punk, and by the looks of him, Mr. Martin wasn't done with him yet.

"What the hell do you think you're doing?" the old man demanded.

"Confessing to a crime," Tate said.

Mr. Martin banged his cane onto the floor three times, then glared. "No! You have no right to confess to something you didn't do. You're trying to be the big hero, and you don't want her hurt." Apparently, he was sharper than he let on.

Madi looked up at Tate. "*Is* that what you're doing?"

Before he could respond, the older man rose to his full five-eight height and said, "It was me. *I* took the meds." He eyeballed the entire crowd in the diner. "Not this—" he gestured toward Tate with his cane "—*punk*. He didn't take the pills. That was me."

"No." A young woman stood from a table across the room. The clerk from the grocery store. "It was me. I was at the clinic for birth control. *I* took them."

"Liars." This came from Mr. Ryan, at the far end of the counter. "We all know I have a problem. It was me."

Madi gaped as the entire town rallied around her. Tate had never seen anything like it.

Luna wolf-whistled loud to get everyone's attention. "Hey, I was there, too. I took the pills."

Madi glanced at her friend. "You weren't there—"

"Oh, no, you don't!" Mr. Martin yelled. "Listen all you—egocentric, self-absorbed, narcissistic group of *insane* people. Don't make me smack all of you!"

And with that, he pulled a small box from his pocket. A sample of OxyContin.

"See?" He held it up triumphantly. "I have them. I have them all. I took them because I thought they were for my constipation. It's the same color. My insurance is crap, and even if it wasn't, I hate to wait in line at the pharmacy!"

Before Madi could respond, a huge squeal sounded, followed by a *whoosh* as the overhead sprinkler system came on out of nowhere, raining down on the entire diner and everyone in it.

CHAPTER TWENTY-ONE

TOTAL CHAOS REIGNED as the sprinklers drenched the diner with icy water. People yelled and screamed, pushing and shoving to get out. Adding to the insanity, the decorations hanging from the ceiling soaked up the water and fell, pulling down the tiles with them. A papier-mâché turkey hit Madi on the head. She saw stars for a second. Someone would get seriously hurt in this mess. She blinked through the downpour to check the crowd for anyone needing assistance but could hardly see two feet in front of her through the frigid torrents. *Everyone* needed help. People were either running or down for the count. Utter mayhem.

Madi gulped a breath and swiped her wet hair out of her face. Her hand came away bloody. She was bleeding. Then she was grabbed and steamrollered her toward the door.

Tate.

"Forget me," she said, struggling against his steely grip. "Get Mr. Martin and Lucille!"

"You first." He dumped her outside, then went back in for more people.

Soon he returned with Mr. Martin and sat the old man down beside Madi on the curb. Lucille was nowhere to be seen though. Mark shoved Luna and Cassie out the door, then went back in for others alongside Tate.

She couldn't just sit there. She had to help. So, despite Tate's wishes, she dove back into the chaos. The sprinklers still poured down water. Madi herded several more people outside before she ran into Tate again. He had two of Lucille's blue-haired posse by the hand, but he stopped to stroke the wet hair out of Madi's face to check her bloody cheek, making sure she was okay.

Warmth washed through her, knowing he cared. It was in his every touch, every look.

And he was still going to leave.

By the time the fire department arrived and shut off the sprinkler system, everyone had been evacuated. Several people were injured enough to require a visit to the ER, and Madi helped triage those people on the sidewalk. Near her, Mark and Tate assisted the paramedics. Mr. Ryan had gotten a nasty laceration down one arm, and Tate was crouched at the vet's side, applying pressure to the wound.

Brock was on the scene now too and rushed first to Cassie's side, then once reassured, moved on to Mr. Ryan.

"He's in shock," Tate said quietly.

It was true. The veteran shook, looking glassy-eyed and disoriented. Brock went to his car and returned with a medical kit. Together, he and Tate wrapped Mr. Ryan in an emergency blanket to get him warm until an ambulance could take him to Wyckford General. Madi helped get the vet settled inside the rig, then jumped back down to assist other people in time to hear the tail end of a conversation between them.

"The least you can do is consider the position," Brock said to Tate. "You're the perfect person to be flight crew team lead. We'd be lucky to have you. And look at all this. We can be exciting for an adrenaline junkie like you too."

Tate shook his head, then crouched at Lucille's feet as Brock stalked off to help another patient.

Madi moved in to ask Lucille, "Are you okay?"

"Oh, sure, honey." The older woman patted her arm, then gazed at Tate adoringly. "He's a good boy."

Tate smiled, then tended to Madi's wounded cheek. "You need that taken care of. Let me—"

"It can wait." She sank to the curb as the crowd began to disperse, dropping her head to her knees, exhausted to the bone and far too close to losing it. Tate ran a big, warm hand down her back, then wrapped an emergency blanket around her.

"I'm fine," Madi muttered.

He sat at her other side and pulled her in against his warmth. "That's not what's in question here."

She lifted her head. "I don't get why you don't trust yourself—you just saved the entire town."

He shrugged. "Probably for the same reason you quit your job. Old demons are hard to beat."

She looked away, and he tugged on her ponytail until she met his gaze again.

"Madi," he said softly. "Please don't do this."

Suddenly, it was all too much. The clinic, the diner, Tate knowing how she felt about him and his leaving anyway. Her head hurt. Her cheek hurt. Her heart hurt too. When her eyes filled with tears, Tate kept his arms around her, and she buried her face in the crook of his neck.

How had things gotten so out of control?

All she'd wanted was to stretch her wings. Live for herself for once instead of for others. "I screwed up," she said into his chest. "I always wished I could go a little crazy, but as it turns out, I'm not a good rebel."

"I think you're better at it than you give yourself credit for."

She choked out a laugh. "I just wanted something for myself."

"You deserve that," Tate said with absolute conviction. From the beginning, he'd treated her like someone special. He'd shared his courage, his sense of adventure, his inner strength. Once, she'd been out of sync with herself and her hopes and dreams. That had changed. Because of him.

She was in balance now, but it wasn't enough.

Loving him wasn't enough either because he was going back to the Air Force, and she'd be alone. Again. The smart thing to do would be to cut her losses before it got worse, but how could she? "Tate."

He looked into her eyes and time seemed to slow.

"I love you." She covered his lips with her fingers when he started to interrupt. "Don't worry, I know you don't feel the same, and I know I screwed up because this was all supposed to be a fling, but I can't do this anymore. I'm sorry."

"Are you dumping me?" His whisper sounded sharp and brittle.

Madi shook her head. "You were never mine to dump."

He nodded and stroked his thumb over her cheekbone in a gentle gesture that made her ache. Madi started to say something more, but someone tapped her on the shoulder.

"Madison Michelle Scott."

Her mother. The only person who ever used her middle name. She stood, and Tate wisely wandered over to talk to Mark and Brock.

"I heard about the diner on the radio in the ER and I came to help." Her mother took Madi's chin in her fingers to assess her cheek. "You're hurt? And you quit your job?" Her mother stared at her for a long beat, during which Madi did her best not to look as utterly heartbroken as she felt. Finally, her mom nodded. "Well, they overworked you anyway."

"You're not upset?" Madi was taken aback.

"The hospital has taken advantage of your skills for years. The board's already banding together to get you back. I suggest you turn them down. According to what I overheard the second offer will be a much better deal."

She choked out a shocked breath. "Mom!"

"I'm proud of you, honey. And now I need to go invite that nice young man of yours over for dinner tonight. He's been good to you. I want to thank him. You go home and take a hot shower and put something on your cut cheek."

Her mother hugged her tight, then pushed her toward her car.

Madi took a last look at the scene. Firefighters were hauling water damaged items out of the wrecked diner.

"Madi?" Brock waved her over to where Mr. Martin still sat huddled on the curb. "He's refusing to go to the hospital. He doesn't have any serious wounds requiring ER treatment. Mostly, he's just shaken up. If you're leaving, could you maybe drive him home?"

In the end, Madi ended up chauffeuring the entire senior posse since Lucille was the only one of them still in possession of her license, and she'd gone to the ER for X-rays. It took nearly an hour to drop everyone off because they all took forever to say their goodbyes and get out of the car. When Madi had finally gotten rid of them all, she drove to Tate's instead.

Still working on adrenaline, frustration and a pain so real it felt like maybe her heart had split in two, she stormed into his open garage and over to where he stood at his worktable. "Are you coming to dinner at my mom's?"

He looked at her, not commenting on what had to be her ghoulish appearance. She'd been hit with the sprinklers, then dust from the ceiling tiles, and now the whole mess had dried into a white, sticky paste that covered her pretty much everywhere.

"I am," he said. "Is that a problem?"

"Yes, it's a problem!"

"Why? I didn't want to be rude. And she said she'd make meatloaf. I don't think I've ever had home-cooked meatloaf. I thought it was a suburban myth."

Madi had never wanted to both hug and strangle someone at the same time before. He was killing her. She pressed the heels of her hands to her eyes but couldn't rub the ache away. Spinning on her heel, she stalked out of the garage, but Tate caught her at her car, pulling her back to him. Madi felt the rumble of his chest and realized he was laughing at her. At least until he saw her face. Then his smile faded.

With a frustrated growl, Madi shoved him away and got into her car. But before she could shut the door, Tate blocked it by crouching beside her, his muscled thighs flexing under the worn denim of his jeans, his expression unreadable. "Why are you shutting me out?"

"That's rich," she managed, throat inexplicably tight. "Coming from you."

He studied her for a long moment. "You don't really love me, Madi. You love this town. You love all these people. And they all love you."

Madi dropped her head to the steering wheel. "Don't tell me what I feel. I know my heart and I know I'll be okay."

"You'll be so much more than okay. You're the strongest woman I've ever met, Madi."

"I'm not strong at all. I thought I could save everyone if I was good enough. That if I was good, nothing bad would happen."

Tate's stroked his hand up and down her back, calming her. "And how did that work out for you?"

She tightened her grip on the steering wheel like it was her only anchor in a spinning world. Nothing was working out. Not her job. Not the way she wanted people to see her. And not things with Tate.

"It wasn't your fault. You did the best you could. Stop carrying all the responsibility for everyone else," he said quietly. "Let it go and be whoever the hell you want to be."

She looked at him a long beat, then asked, "What about you?"

"What about me?"

"Are you going to take your own advice?"

Rather than answer her question, Tate pulled Madi from the car, then led her inside. After making sure she took a nice hot shower to remove the caked-on dust covering her from head to toe, he wrapped her in a towel and sat her on the counter. He rooted around in a drawer and came up with a first aid kit, which he set near her hip.

Then he pushed her wet hair from her face and eyed the cut on her cheek. He disinfected the area, and when she hissed in pain, he leaned in and kissed her temple.

"Nice bedside manner," she murmured. "You kiss all your patients like that?"

"Almost never." He smiled as he carefully peeled back the plastic packaging on a pack of sterilized butterfly bandages and used them to cover her wound.

"Have you reenlisted already?" she asked.

"Not yet. I left a message for my detachment officer, that's all."

He continued tending to her, concentrating on his task and leaving her free to stare at him. His mouth looked both stern and generous at the same time, his jaw square and rough with a day's worth of scruff she knew would feel deliciously sensual against her skin. A tiny scar marred one side of his face and another on his temple, signs of a life filled with adventure and danger.

"Do you miss it?" she said softly. "The action."

"Once an adrenaline junkie, always one, I guess." He finished with the cut on her face, then lifted her hand, turning it over to gently probe her swollen wrist.

"It's not broken," she said.

He nodded, brushing a kiss over her bruised skin before expertly wrapping it in an Ace bandage. Then he moved on to her bleeding shin. She hadn't even realized she was hurt there.

"Why did you stay so long?" she asked.

He looked up into her face. "I think you know why."

There were some advantages to changing her life, to living for herself instead of for the expectations of others. For one thing, it gave her new confidence. She accessed some of that now by unwrapping the towel around her and letting it fall to the counter at her hips.

Tate went still, and a sensual thrill rushed through her.

He let out a breath and slid his hands up her legs, his fingers rough and strong but tender at the same time, and she quivered, rejoicing in the rightness of his touch. He murmured something against her skin and Madi urged him on, clutching at his shoulders until her toes curled, until she cried out his name, until there were no more thoughts.

Tate had wanted to get his hands on Madi again since he'd heard about the missing drugs from Mark. Hell, he'd been wanting to put his hands on her since—well—*always*.

As they sprawled in his bed later, he stared up at the ceiling, trying to figure out what the hell to do while Madi snoozed beside him.

"Tate?" she murmured; her voice groggy with sleep.

He ran his fingers through her hair and drowned in her eyes. "Yeah?"

"I meant it when I said I loved you."

He knew that too. Knew it to the depths of his soul.

He'd been a military brat who'd never landed in one place for long, then a soldier himself. After the accident he'd steered clear of anything that even remotely sounded like a real connection. He was fine with that. Or so he'd thought.

Until Madi…

In his heart of hearts, he'd known from the first stormy night that his tie to her had been undeniable and unbreakable, no matter how he might have wished otherwise. It'd happened in an instant and had only strengthened with time. Tate couldn't imagine a future without her now. Talking, touching, kissing—whatever he could get because she beat back the darkness inside him. But being with her was also a double-edged sword. Because every minute he spent with Madi absolutely changed his definitions of—*everything*.

She made him feel differently about the past. Made him realize, hope, maybe that tragic night in the ocean hadn't been his fault. That maybe he'd been caught up in circumstances beyond his control and he'd done the best he could with what he was given. Madi also made Tate yearn for things he'd not experienced in a long time—home, family, love. She made him yearn to put down roots and make a life for himself. With her. Here in Wyckford.

His entire universe had gone topsy-turvy and that scared him most of all.

The only thing he was certain of was being with her felt right. *Real.* "Careful." He shifted slightly to kiss her swollen cheek, then her wrapped wrist. "Don't hurt yourself."

Madi smiled, then nuzzled into his side again and went back to sleep.

Her hair was in his face, her body plastered to his. She had one leg thrown over him, her face stuck to his pec, her hand over his heart like she owned it.

She did own it. His soul too.

Jesus. All this had started out so innocuously. Innocent, even.

Okay, not innocent. But that night at the auction he'd not been in a good place. Hadn't felt good enough for his own life, much less anyone else's. Certainly not for a woman like Madi, who'd give a perfect stranger the shirt off her back.

But being with her made him feel good.

Worthy.

He'd never intended to be anything to her except a good time, but best-laid plans…

Maybe he should've run hard and fast that first night, but something about her had drawn him in.

His arms involuntarily tightened around her, and although Madi gave a soft sigh and cuddled deeper into him, she didn't waken. Nor did she stir when Tate forced himself to let her go and slip out of bed. He needed some time to think and work out his next steps. But first, there was something else he had to do. And he had to do it alone.

Madi awakened slowly, thinking about the day before—the clinic being shut down, her quitting, the chaos at the diner—and Tate making it all okay. Responsive but not smothering, encouraging her to talk when necessary and letting her be quiet when it'd counted.

She stretched, her muscles aching in a very delicious way.

In truth, it hadn't been just sex for her since their first time, but she hadn't been sure how he felt.

Until last night.

The way he'd touched her, the way he'd looked at her, how he'd responded, had been lovemaking at its finest. Smiling, she rolled over and reached for him, but found only an empty mattress.

Something inside her went cold.

She sat up and grabbed her phone off the night-stand. A text flashed on-screen. She squinted, thinking it might be Tate—maybe he got called in for a shift—but it was from Judith:

The board refused your resignation. The clinic is back open. Your next shift is tomorrow at eight. See you then!

Wrapping herself in a sheet, she walked through the house, searching for Tate, but he was gone.

Madi got to the garage and flipped on the light. The Chevelle was missing too.

Heart in her throat, she ran back to the bedroom to get dressed, then figure out what the hell was going on. He couldn't leave now. She wouldn't let him. But first she had to find him.

She'd just finished putting on her shoes when she noticed something on the floor. A small, care-fully wrapped gift. It must've been knocked off the nightstand when she'd reached for her phone. Madi picked it up.

Pulse racing and face hot, she sank down on the edge of the bed to open it. Inside was the brace-let she'd so coveted from the charity auction all those weeks ago. She had no idea how Tate had known she'd even wanted it, but maybe he'd overheard her talking with Mr. Martin that night in the lobby…

Tears stung her eyes as she stared down at it. He'd even added another charm to it, this one of a car that looked suspiciously like the Chevelle. That was it. That was all she needed to know.

Throat tight, she put it on and shored up her determination to continue stretching her wings. She'd done as she'd wanted. She'd stepped out of her comfort zone. She'd lived her life the way she saw fit, and it'd been more exciting than she could've imagined.

But how did she go back to being her old self again?

You don't.

She'd laid her heart on the line for the first time in her life, and Tate loved her, even if he might not admit it. To her or to himself. And she refused to let that go.

Not yet.

Maybe not ever, if she had her way.

CHAPTER TWENTY-TWO

TATE SAT IN an uncomfortable chair in front of Bud Lofton, administrator, and head of the board of directors for Wyckford General Hospital. He'd faced down the worst firefights and snipers in the world during his time in the Air Force, but he'd never felt more nervous in his life. He resisted the urge to fidget as the other man assessed him from across the desk.

"Tell me why we should hire you as permanent leader for the flight paramedic team," Bud said, holding the résumé Tate had hastily put together before he'd left his house earlier. "I know what's on here, and your work for us thus far speaks for itself, but tell me what's not on this résumé. Tell me who you are, Tate Griffin."

On his first mission, and on every assignment up to the accident, Tate had thrived on what he'd been doing. He'd believed in his work and understood he'd belonged out saving lives. After the crash, he hadn't just lost four friends. He'd also lost something of himself. His ability to connect. To get attached. His trust in his instincts.

Until the nosy, pestering people of this small town, who cared about everyone and everything in their path. Including him.

And Madi. She'd been the last piece of his shattered soul fitting back into place.

Tate cleared his throat, then said, "I'm a hard worker, dependable, loyal. I've got the experience and the drive and the knowledge to lead this team, and I have the foresight to keep it going to serve the people of Wyckford and the surrounding areas. I promise you that while there might be a few hiccups on the way and things might not always be perfect, I will always strive to do the best I can in every situation, sir."

Bud watched him closely for a moment, then picked up another paper from his desk. "I have a letter here from Dr. Brock Turner, speaking very highly of your capabilities and skills as a paramedic. He recommends you for the job."

Not sure what to say about that, Tate just nodded.

"And another from one of our firefighters, Mark Bates. He too gives you a glowing review."

For the first time in four years, Tate's chest tightened with something other than stress when he realized these people had gotten close to him. They knew him and cared about him, and he about them. He forced words out of his suddenly constricted throat. "Thank you, sir."

Since the accident, he'd thought keeping people

away would help him forget and keep him safe. But now he knew the opposite was true. Being alone had only made him miserable.

Happiness had arrived when he'd come to Wyckford. The town and all the nosy folks here and one special woman who'd destroyed the carefully constructed barriers around his heart.

Brad, Tommy, Kelly, and Trevor's deaths would *always* mean something to him. And maybe forgiveness had to start with himself first. Yes, he'd given the order to go on that rescue mission that night, knowing the conditions, knowing how dangerous it was. But Madi was right. His team had known all the risks and they'd still chosen to follow him. They wouldn't want Tate to suffer endlessly for a decision made with no good choices available. They'd want him to be happy. Deep down, he'd probably always known that, but he hadn't had his head screwed on straight for a long time. It was now.

"No need to thank me." Bud stood and extended his hand to Tate. "Especially since you're going to have your hands full with the new flight crew. Congratulations and we're glad to welcome you as a permanent member of the Wyckford General Hospital. HR will contact you to sign all the paperwork."

Tate left the interview more determined than ever. He'd gotten his professional life back on track.

Now to focus on the personal one.

Driving past the parking lot of the Buzzy Bird Café, Tate saw the café was boarded up, but there were still a few cars there, people helping to clean the place up and get it back open again in time for Thanksgiving next week.

Heart pounding, Tate parked, then walked to the entrance. Amidst the wreckage from the sprinklers, he spotted Luna and Cassie and Madi near the counter, mops and brooms in hand.

He stepped inside and all three women turned his way. Madi froze, the charm bracelet glinting on her wrist.

Tate had absolutely no idea what she was thinking since her expression was carefully blank.

A lesson she'd probably learned from him.

CHAPTER TWENTY-THREE

MADI STARED AT TATE, her breath held.

He wore dress pants and a white button-down shirt with a tie, looking very professional.

Heart pounding, she said to her friends, "Give us a minute, please."

Luna looked at him, using her first two fingers to point at him, going back and forth between his eyes and hers, silently giving him notice she was watching and not to even *think* about misbehaving.

Cassie dragged Luna through the door leading into the kitchen.

Madi waited until they were out of earshot, then walked over to where he stood near the door. Her entire being went warm as she drank in the sight of him.

"You still trying to save me?" he asked quietly once she reached him.

She shrugged. "I can't seem to help myself."

"I don't need saving."

No. No, he didn't. He was strong and capable and more than able to take care of himself. "What *do* you need?"

"You," he said simply. "Only you."

"Oh," Cassie said softly through the kitchen pass-through window. "That's good."

"So good," Luna agreed.

Madi turned and glared at her friends until they disappeared again.

"Sorry." She refocused on Tate. He took her hand in his, entwining their fingers and bringing them to his chest, his heartbeat a reassuring steady thump beneath her palm. "I know you've looked for a hero," he said. "But how about a regular guy?"

Her throat went tight. "That'd be great. But I don't see any regular guys in front of me."

The corner of his mouth tipped up, but she wasn't going to be distracted by his hotness yet. "What about your reenlistment?"

"I thought that's what I wanted, but I was wrong. The only thing I want now is you, Madi. *You* fulfill me. You make me whole. You're the greatest rush I've ever known."

Sniffling echoed from the kitchen.

She ignored it, even as her own tears welled. "Does this mean you're staying?"

"It does. Bud Lofton just hired me permanently as the flight crew team leader. And I'd also like to volunteer to run some of the veterans' programs at the clinic too, if it's still going."

Madi absorbed all this with what felt like a huge bucket of hope on her chest. "It's still going."

Tate smiled, his voice sounding raw and staggered and touched beyond words as he said, "God, I was so stupid, Madi. I didn't know what to do with you. I tried to keep my distance, but my world doesn't work without you in it."

She melted. And given the twin sighs echoing from the kitchen, Madi wasn't the only one.

Tate cupped her cheek, careful of her wound, then kissed her. "I love you too, Madi," he said very quietly. "So damn much." Then his eyes went dark as he murmured against her lips, "How do you feel about sealing the deal with a ring?"

"What?" she squeaked, pulling back. "You want to get engaged? To be *married*?"

"You're it for me." Tate tipped her chin up and looked deep into her eyes, and there she found the truth. He stroked a finger over her temple, tucking a loose strand of hair behind her ear. "The best choice I ever made."

"Yes!" Heart full to bursting, Madi kissed the man she'd spend forever with.

* * * * *